MIA'S RIDING CAMP

Anna Sellberg

Mia's Riding Camp

Translated by Kjell Johansson
Typeset by Roberta L. Melzl
Editor: Bobbie Chase
Printed in Germany, 2008

ISBN: 978-1-933343-85-3

Stabenfeldt, Inc.
457 North Main Street
Danbury, CT 06811
www.pony4kids.com

Available exclusively through PONY Book Club.

CHAPTER 1

A shrill sound woke Mia. Still in her dream world, she tried to shut the alarm off, but instead pushed the clock from her night table, making it fall to the floor with a thud. It kept ringing even louder.

Mia threw her comforter off, dove to the floor and found the clock. Finally, it was silent and Mia sighed with relief. She yawned deeply, stretched her entire body and sat on the edge of the bed. Then she remembered what day this was and suddenly was very awake. She looked at the clock again. Six thirty. In just two hours, she and Burly would be on their way to the Edinburgh Riding Camp!

With her stomach full of butterflies Mia stood up and went to the memo board above the little white desk. Next to a photo of Burly's head was a little ad that she'd cut from a horse magazine a few months ago. She read the ad for the thousandth time.

"Come to the Edinburgh Riding Camp, the camp for horse owners. Practice jumping and dressage with our experienced instructors for five wonderful summer days. Welcome!"

"Mia, are you awake?"

Mia's mom knocked gently on the door before opening it, and Mia nodded.

"Yes, I'll just get dressed."

"Dad's milking the cows now. If you're going to be there by nine, we'd better start loading soon. I've already groomed Burly and taken his blanket out. Let's just hope he behaves."

Mia sighed. "Don't worry, Mom. Burly is great at being loaded. He's been in trailers before, you know."

"You can never be too sure," Mia's mom said and yawned. "I'll make breakfast now."

She left and Mia heard her footsteps disappear down the stairs. She had sounded nervous. In truth, her mom used to ride and groom Burly every once in a while, but she had always had a wary respect for him. Burly isn't very tall, just about 57 inches at the withers, but he's a

6

sturdy Norwegian Fjord horse and he knows just exactly how strong he is!

It had been a long time since Mia stopped trying to win Burly over with pure strength. It was just impossible. She had to be smarter than he, and of course more stubborn. That wasn't always easy, and in the beginning Burly had won more than once, but over time he had actually gained some respect for the obstinate human who never gave up, no matter how much he fussed.

Nowadays Mia had almost forgotten how troublesome Burly could be when he wanted to.

Mia stood in the bathroom, pulling a brush through her short blonde hair. She made a face at her own image. Her gray eyes looked serious and she was irritated when she saw a new zit on her chin.

"Are you ready yet?" her dad called from the hall. "We have to leave now!"

"I'm coming," Mia answered, and after a last look at the ill-timed zit she hurried out to the barn.

Burly was tied outside his stall and neighed quietly when he saw Mia. Mia quickly patted his neck and gave him a couple of sugar cubes.

"I put his thin cotton blanket on, so he won't be cold in the trailer," Mia's mom said, pushing her glasses up on her nose.

"And he has the trailer guards that Grandma and Grandpa gave you for your birthday. Our little boy actually looks like a real competition horse," she proudly went on.

Mia sighed silently. Sometimes her mom was sillier than she had the right to be when it came to Burly.

She quickly loaded saddle, bridle and the rest of Burly's equipment in the car. Her bag with her clothes was already in the luggage compartment, next to her helmet, her riding boots and the crop. Now it was time to load Burly.

Mia went into the stable and Burly looked at her with ears pricked. His dark eyes had a curious glint. *He must be wondering what's going on*, Mia thought. She caressed his muzzle before loosening the lead rein. He seemed as calm as ever, but Mia was so nervous she was dry in the mouth.

Not because of Burly. She was sure he would manage fine at Edinburgh. No, she was nervous for herself. Would she make it? Would she manage to get to know lots of new people whom she'd never met before, and feel comfortable sleeping in a strange bed, away from home for almost a week? She hardly dared open her mouth in school usually, and always had trouble sleeping away from home, and…

Just suppose she didn't make any friends at all? Mia bitterly knew how it felt to be outside the cool gang, not allowed in. Although she had been in the same school from first to sixth grade, it wasn't until last fall, when she started seventh grade at a school in town and gotten a bunch of new classmates, that she had finally made her first real friends.

In her old class, she had been the little shy gray

mouse – not a total loner, but certainly not one of the in-crowd, either.

Now she had her friend Tessa, who also rode and loved horses, but who was in Italy at the moment with her parents. Tessa had wanted to go to the riding camp too, but her parents had said no. Their trip to Italy had been planned for a long time and couldn't be changed. Right now, more than anything, Mia longed for Tessa to be here, sitting on the oats box and dangling her legs as she usually did.

Mia took a deep breath and grabbed Burly's head collar. Just then one of the cows mooed and a couple more followed her example. All the cows in the nearest row turned their heads and gave Burly, with his neat appearance, curious looks. He wasn't his usual self, the muddy, loves-to-roll Fjord horse they usually walked with out in the paddock, Mia thought. She swallowed although she had nothing to swallow.

She realized that more than anything, she wanted to let Burly out in the pen and forget about all this! She would have given almost anything to not have to go away and meet a lot of strangers who were sure to laugh at her and her Fjord horse. She knew what those competition people were like. They always rode fancy purebreds, which cost hundreds of thousands and could jump anything. Of course, they also had more money than you could imagine.

She was sure Burly would be the only Fjord horse at the camp, and she had only ridden at home and jumped her own obstacles with Tessa. She had also only been in competitions twice…

"Mia! Hurry!" her dad called from the door. "We have to leave now, or you'll be late!"

"I'm on my way. Come on, Burly, let's go," Mia said with a strangely tense voice that was quite different from her usual tone.

Burly nudged at her softly with his muzzle, as if he wanted to cheer her up, and then they went out into the yard where the car and trailer waited.

Rain fell quietly but stubbornly from the lead-gray sky and Mia felt herself shudder when she and Burly came out of the stable. It was the middle of June, but it felt more like November. All over the yard were big pools of water in the gravel, but Mia didn't regret not wearing her rubber boots. They were so totally ugly: old, green and reeking of cow. She preferred getting her feet wet in her cool brown riding shoes.

When Burly saw the trailer he hesitated and stopped, and then raised his head and pricked his ears as he studied it.

"He'll never go in," Mia's mom said, worried, and pushed on Burly's round hindquarters. "Come on, boy, it's not dangerous! Come on now."

"Stop it, Mom," Mia said, trying her best not to sound irritated. "He just wants to look at it a little first."

"Shouldn't we get the ropes? Maybe that would be best. We don't have that much time," her mom said, patting Burly again.

"Stop it," Mia hissed, unable to hide her irritation any longer. "He'll go in. I promise."

"It's all right, hon," Mia's dad said, removing his glasses and drying them with a handkerchief. "Burly's a smart horse. He knows the score."

"Yes, but…" Mom began, but she was interrupted by Burly, who suddenly decided to walk forward. Without further ado he went straight into the trailer, which rocked and creaked under his weight. Snorting contently, he buried his muzzle in the trailer's hay net and happily started eating his second breakfast while Mia tied him.

"Thanks," she whispered into his soft ear. "We're leaving now. This will be a lot of fun!"

She knew she'd said the last sentence mostly to cheer herself up. Still, it felt comforting to hear herself say it. After all, she had chosen to go to the camp. She had even had to persuade her parents for days before they agreed to let her go. She couldn't bail out now, Mia thought as she jumped out of the trailer and shut the little front door behind her.

"Are you ready to go?" her dad asked, and Mia nodded.

"Good luck, honey," her mom said and gave her a quick hug. "Promise you'll call, and don't forget to…"

"Mom! I'll only be gone for a week. It's going to be all right," Mia interrupted, quickly getting into the car before her mom had time to say anything more.

The engine started and Burly stepped a little back and

11

forth, making the trailer rock. Mia fastened her seat belt. Then she waved merrily and forced herself to smile at her mom, who still looked a little worried.

When the car passed the pen Mia looked at the obstacles; the thin bars she used for poles, the oil barrels and the old chairs. Everything looked very worn, gray and pitiful in the rain.

Mia set her jaw and looked through the windscreen of the car, where the wipers pushed raindrops away with long, even sweeps.

What had she gotten herself into?

CHAPTER 2

Mia's first impression of Edinburgh was that it was big. The avenue leading up to the farm was almost a mile long and lined with old knotty trees with huge tops. In the pens she could see more horses than she had time to count. Most of them were probably trotters, Mia guessed. She had heard that Edinburgh was famous for its trotters. When they came into the yard she saw a big white stable, and next to it was a riding ring with obstacles in lots of colors – all of them extremely high. A little further away was something that looked like an indoor ring.

The stable was big, bright and clean enough for a person to live in, Mia thought as she led Burly through the door. He looked around with interest and Mia could tell he was surprised. This was very different from the barn at home where he'd been living for the past three years. Before that, he had lived with the old man who raised him and where he'd shared a small dark barn with a lot of sheep and several bulls.

"Are you wondering where the cows are?" Mia whispered. The thought that cows would live in this luxurious stable made her want to laugh.

"Hi there! You can take that stall over there."

A guy in his early thirties, with blond, short-cropped hair and dressed in jeans and a dirty white T-shirt, stepped out of a stall in front of her. He had a pitchfork in his hand and there was a very full wheelbarrow by the stall door. The guy pointed to a nice corner stall with windows on two sides at the end of the passageway, and Mia obediently led Burly inside.

In the stall was a thick layer of fragrant sawdust and somebody had put a little hay in one corner.

As soon as Mia took the blanket and the trailer guards off Burly he eagerly went to both windows and looked at the horses outside. He then neighed shrilly and scraped a little with one front hoof.

"He seems to like it here," Mia's dad said with a smile. "I guess I'll have to rebuild the barn at home for him."

Mia nodded.

"Yes, why don't you. That'll give him a nice surprise when we come home."

"Yeah, you'd like that, wouldn't you," her dad grumbled. He glared at her, but in jest, and went to get saddle and bridle.

"I'm Nick, by the way," the guy with the now empty wheelbarrow said, coming back from the dung heap. "I'm Greta's husband. Sorry I didn't come out to say hi, but I didn't even hear you coming. You must be one of the camp girls?"

"Yes, I am. My name is Maria, but I'm called Mia. And this is Burly."

Mia thought that her voice sounded terrible, shrill and tense. She felt tongue-tied and couldn't help blushing. How embarrassing! Imagine not even being able to answer a simple question. What a yokel she was.

In his new stall, Burly had already started on its most important feature: the hay. Nick smiled, a little teasingly.

"He likes food, right?"

"Yes, he does," Mia said. She sighed, thinking about the usual jokes that were sure to come now, about how Fjord horses really should be called fat horses, how they were always way too heavy, couldn't jump, and…

Mia steeled herself. She was ready to defend Burly with her life, but to her great surprise, Nick didn't say any of the things she'd expected. Instead he noted that Burly seemed to be in great shape and that he had nice muscles.

Mia nodded and didn't really know what to say to all

the praise that this stranger had just heaped on her horse. She couldn't help feeling a little relieved. She was just about to say that Burly walked in a pen with just a little grass in it at home, that he was in the stable at night and that she rode him both morning and evening when she had the time, when she was interrupted by a car coming into the yard. From the trailer behind the car you could hear angry thuds and kicks from a horse that obviously didn't like riding in a trailer.

"Ah, there's Kate Bergman," Nick said, smiling. "You can hear them coming for miles. It's a wonder their trailer hasn't fallen apart yet."

"I'll say," Mia's dad said, coming into the stable with Burly's things. "That horse is going to kick a leg through the trailer wall any time now!"

"Don't worry," Nick said. "The trailer is lined with sheet metal on the inside, just in case. By the way, the tack room is in there," he said, pointing to a green door. "I'll go out and ask Kate's mom if they need any help unloading."

Mia and her dad went into the tack room. The place was immaculate. All the leather shone and the floor was newly swept.

"What a place," Mia's dad said in awe. "We've met our match."

He smiled at Mia, who made a face in reply. She'd been nagging him for years to fix up a real tack room for her so she wouldn't have to keep Burly's stuff in a

corner of the barn, but every time he promised to get to it
something else got in the way. Mia hoped that seeing this
room would inspire him, but she guessed the chances
were slim.

Mia could hear a joyous voice babbling from within
the stable, and Nick laughing. She got curious and left the
tack room with her dad in tow. The first thing she saw was
a chubby little girl with frizzy red hair and lots of freckles.
Her eyes were very blue and she seemed to radiate energy.
She wore green, threadbare riding pants and a faded striped
sweater. When the new girl saw Mia, her face lit up.

"Hi! Is this your Fjord horse next to Prince? He's so
cute! He's just getting to know my ruffian, who almost
kicked the trailer to pieces on the way here. I wish I could
understand why he keeps doing that. He's just hopeless!
No matter how often he travels in the trailer, he just keeps
kicking and kicking…"

"Take a breath at some point, honey, so I can go home.
Here, grab your things and I'll get out of here."

A big, hefty woman in a blue-and-white checkered skirt
and a white shirt with a logo that read *Bergman's Wash*
came into the stable, dragging an enormous trunk after her.
Her hair was also red and frizzy, and her red face almost
matched her hair by the time she'd finished dragging the
heavy trunk. Mia realized this must be Kate's mom.

"Okay, okay, I'm coming. I have to say hi, right? By
the way, I'm Kate, but I bet Nick already told you that.
And your name is…?"

Kate looked questioningly at Mia, but Mia hardly had the time to say "Mia" before Kate nodded, turned on her heel and ran out of the stable, almost as quickly as she talked. Mia looked into the stall and a sour-looking chestnut with a broad white blaze and white socks on all four legs, his ears pointing backwards, glared at her.

"I'm sorry I have to go back so soon, but my husband couldn't take the day off as he'd promised," Kate's mom said to Nick, probably to explain why she was in such a hurry. "I have four more kids at home, you know, and the twins will just tear the house apart if I'm out of sight for more than ten minutes," she went on, sighing.

"I understand," Nick said. "I remember how they are… Hey, is your Shetland pony still alive?"

"Yes, it would take more than my kids to finish that pony off," Kate's mom nodded, "and that really is a blessing, you know. But I guess the Society for the Prevention of Cruelty to Animals will come around any day now. The other day, the kids hitched her to their doll carriage and pretended they were at a trotting competition…"

She didn't have to say any more. Nick started laughing, and Mia pictured a fat little pony running around pulling a doll carriage. Actually, the thought was pretty funny, although she felt a little sorry for the pony.

"Now I've got everything," Kate gasped, running along the passageway with saddle, bridle, and a pink bucket that read PRINCE.

She dropped a shocking-pink plastic currycomb, which looked brand new. Nick picked it up with a quiet sigh and put it back in the bucket.

"Bye, honey! Promise me you'll call home every once in a while. And don't go gabbing until Nick and Greta's ears bleed!"

"Yes mom, no mom," Kate answered, ducking in a vain attempt to avoid the loud kiss her mom planted on her cheek.

Then she ran off to the tack room with all her stuff, and the stable was suddenly very quiet.

"Kate the Wild has landed," Nick said with a smile.

Mia nodded. She knew just what he meant, but she also felt that she already liked Kate. Maybe this would be fun!

"What a great room!" Kate exclaimed, cheerfully throwing herself backwards onto one of the beds, which protested with an angry creak.

Mia sat down on her own bed, a little more carefully, and looked around. The room was small but still held two white beds with blue and white striped bedspreads and a bureau with four drawers. On the floor was a rag rug, and on the window, which had a view of a big pasture, were curtains that seemed newly washed.

"You want some candy?" Kate asked, rushing up again and digging in her backpack. "I bought lots at a store on the way here and now I'm starving."

"We should have lunch any second now. It's past

noon. But I wouldn't mind a little candy first," Mia said, catching the bag that Kate threw at her.

"So how do you like the others?" Kate asked.

"I guess they're all right," Mia said. "I've hardly even met them yet. What do you think? You seem to know a few of them."

"Three," Kate nodded and chewed vigorously at a licorice whip. "Ivy and Emma ride in the same group with me every Wednesday. Emma has a Connemara pony named Samson. He can jump anything. Ivy's pony's name is Jolly Gray Delight. I'm sure Ivy's parents must have paid a small fortune for Jolly, but they have lots of money, because her dad owns a great big clothing store. She rides like a clod, but she's really nice."

"Mm," Mia said. "Who else do you know?"

"Linda," Kate said, squinting at Mia. "She's in my class at school. She's the biggest wimp in the world and I didn't even know she had a horse. As long as I've known her, she's only ridden at the riding school."

"So what about Ricky?" Mia asked, catching the bag of candy that Kate threw at her again.

"I've never met Ricky before, and I can't say I'm sorry about that. He looks like a real goody-two-shoes. By the way, did you see that Gotland pony grazing in the pen by the stable? I actually had a Gotland pony before. Her name was Hilda."

"Is she dead now?" Mia said before she had the time to think. Kate stared at her in surprise.

"Yes. How in the world did you know?"

Mia giggled again. "Your mom talked about a poor Shetland pony…"

"Oh, you mean Doll?" Kate sighed. "Mom felt so sorry for Prince, being all alone after Hilda died, that she bought the meanest Shetland pony in the world. We have our own little stable, behind the house, with two stalls. Doll is a real monster. She's cute and all that, but there's not a kid in the world who can sit on her for more than three minutes. But we were talking about something. Do *you* like Ricky?"

"I think he's kind of cute, with that dark curly hair."

Kate snorted.

"Angel's curls. He's not my type. But I wouldn't mind taking his horse home with me."

Mia could only agree. Mistral was a crossbred pony, cream-colored with a white star, and when he moved it was as if he danced.

Just then there was a knock at the door, and a thin brown-haired girl with glasses stuck her head in the room.

"You're just in time, Linda. We were just going to talk about you," Kate said teasingly. Linda blushed.

"I just wanted to ask something," Linda said. "But I'll leave right away."

"No way," Kate said. "Have a seat and grab some candy. Here, try the licorice whips. They're great!"

Linda carefully sat on the edge of a chair. Then she shyly looked down into the bag, as if she expected to find something really gross there instead of candy. After a long moment she picked up one raspberry jellybean and gave the bag back to Kate.

Mia realized that Linda felt a little awkward too. She was glad that there was somebody else who didn't know everything about everything, because although both Kate and Linda seemed really nice, Mia had felt shy and awkward when she said hello to Ricky, Ivy and Emma in the stable. Ivy and Ricky seemed so cool and self-assured, and Mia had learned that Emma was Ivy's best friend. Still, Mia thought that Emma seemed to be the nicest among them. She didn't say very much – she mostly smiled and pushed her long bangs off her face with a little gesture.

Mia felt that she would have a hard time relaxing and being herself with those two girls. And she thought that Ricky was a good-looking guy … Mia felt her stomach tingle when she thought about how he had smiled at her when they were talking in the stable. Kate could say what she wanted, but Mia still thought he seemed really nice.

"Do you know when our first meeting is?" Linda asked.

"They'll come and tell us when it's lunch time. And after lunch they'll show us around the farm and tell us a little more about what we'll be practicing during the course," Kate said quickly. Mia wondered how she could know all that.

"Have you met Greta?" Mia asked Linda, who shook her head.

22

"Our riding teacher? No, but that guy in the stable said she'd join us for lunch. He's her husband. Have you ridden here before?" Linda said, looking at Mia.

Mia shook her head.

"No, never. I've mostly ridden alone at home, and I have a friend who rides at the riding school in town. She helps me with Burly. I'm certainly no expert."

Linda nodded and seemed relieved.

"That's good to hear," she said. "I've been so scared. I've had Graygirl just a little while, and before that I only rode at a riding school, like you. What if we all make fools of ourselves? Is Greta nice, or does she yell at you all the time?"

"She's so nice you can feel sorry for her," Kate said, smiling before she went on, "So why didn't you tell me you'd bought a horse? I was very surprised when I saw you here."

"I didn't want to say anything before I knew that it was all going to work out," Linda said. "I have Graygirl at my grandpa's place for now. She's stabled with his two trotters. But this fall, I've been promised a stall in a little stable closer to town. Then I can see her every day."

"Well, your own horse is nothing to keep secret," Kate exclaimed. "And you can stop worrying about making a fool of yourself. Do you know how many faults Prince and I had last time we jumped a course? Twenty-nine and a half! The judge almost had a stroke when Prince dragged the entire last obstacle with him just because he didn't feel like lifting his legs."

Linda and Mia laughed. Just then there was a knock at the door and a girl in her mid-twenties opened it and looked in. She was dressed in jeans and a blue-checked shirt, wore glasses and had long blonde hair in a ponytail. Mia immediately felt that she liked her. She looked so kind and nice.

"Hi! So here you are. I'm Greta. I know you from before, Kate, but who are you two? Linda and Maria?"

"Call me Mia," Mia quickly said. "Everybody does."

"And I'm Linda," Linda piped up.

"Okay, come on now, girls, let's have lunch. Later, when we've digested our food and had a look at the farm, we'll have the first lesson."

Mia swallowed and looked at Linda, who seemed every bit as nervous as she herself felt. Ouch. It was almost time to show what she and Burly were worth. Once again, Mia wished she had never come up with the idea of going to this riding camp.

CHAPTER 3

Many hours later, Mia was tossing and turning in bed. She couldn't sleep, although she was so tired that her entire body ached. Kate was already sleeping soundly in her bed. She seemed to have fallen asleep as soon as she laid her head on the pillow.

Mia felt homesickness creeping in. She turned over again with a sigh. No, she just couldn't sleep. Instead, she lay there thinking about what had happened during the day.

Lunch had been great, although Mia had been so

nervous that she hardly ate. When she saw that Linda was just pushing her food around on her plate too she immediately felt better. At least they could be worried together!

Ricky, Ivy, Emma and Kate had babbled away together almost the entire time. They seemed to know everybody and everything about everybody: who owned which horse, who had won which competition, etcetera…

In the beginning Mia tried to keep up with their chatter, but she soon gave up. She didn't know any of the people anyway, although she had seen a few of the names in different horse magazines.

After lunch, Greta had started talking about Edinburgh, and the others had fallen silent. All in all, there were thirty-five trotters at Edinburgh, ranging from foals that were just a couple of months old to full-grown competition horses. Greta's dad and Nick took care of the trotters along with three hired stable hands, while Greta looked after the riding horses. She didn't have a formal riding school, but just held practice sessions for people with their own horses. She also took care of breaking in horses and things like that.

"What a great place to live," Linda had whispered to Mia when they were walking around the stables to have a look a while later.

"Absolutely," Mia said and nodded.

This was exactly what she wanted in the future: her own farm and lots of horses to care for. So far it was only a dream, but she decided to try to learn as much as she could during her week here.

They walked everywhere and looked at everything. The trotters had their own stable a bit further off from the riding horses, in three rows of big stalls. Mia silently counted them. Forty stalls.

In an enormous stall of a little stable all his own was the pride of the stud farm, the trotting stallion Speedy O'Boy, and Mia thought to herself that his stall was as big as their living room at home. Speedy O'Boy actually didn't look that special – he just seemed like an ordinary brown horse, as he stood half-sleeping in a corner. It was hard for Mia to imagine that he was one of the fastest trotters in the world.

The riders then went on to the riding horse stable, where their own six ponies were in their stalls. Greta showed them the feed room, the tack room and the manure pile, and then everybody got to say a few words about themselves and their horses.

Mia hardly knew what to say. After Ivy and Ricky had talked about all the competitions they had won and it was her turn, it felt a little silly to say that she and Burly had only started in two Easy D competitions and nothing more. She stammered something about wanting to learn more, and that she wanted to be in competitions again this fall, and then it was thankfully Kate's turn to talk about herself and Prince.

Mia sighed and turned over in bed. Why did she have

to be so shy! She really envied Kate, who seemed to be able to laugh at everything and everybody. Kate didn't seem afraid of anything – not even her angry horse Prince could frighten her.

Mia had watched as Kate cheerfully groomed and took care of Prince earlier in the day, impressed. Prince's ears had been stuck back the whole time, and he snapped at the air as far as his lead rein would allow. He looked like a sly, mean snake. And he looked ready to kick at any moment. He stamped his hind legs in irritation, and a couple of times he kicked hard at the stall wall, making Mia and Burly jump.

Mia couldn't understand why Kate wasn't afraid.

"Pshaw," Kate said a while later when they had mounted and were heading for the riding ring. "Prince is just fooling around. If he'd been born human, I'm sure they would have given him an Academy Award for playing the meanest villain in the world by now, but the fact is he's incredibly ticklish, especially on his stomach. That's why he keeps jumping and fussing. If you look closely, you'll see that he always kicks with the leg that's on the other side from me, and when he snaps in the air, he never means to bite for real."

"But hasn't he ever bitten you by mistake?" Mia asked.

Kate giggled.

"Yes, once," she said. "And then he was so embarrassed he had his ears forward for an entire week. Right, boy?"

She affectionately stroked her chestnut along his neck

and he turned an ear back to listen to her before he pricked them again.

Mia looked around as they walked the course. Linda was walking calmly on Graygirl with long reins, just as Mia was doing on Burly, but Mistral didn't want to walk and Ricky was sitting with short reins, stiff and straight-backed. Mistral jig-jogged with quick short steps and kept tossing his head, although he wore a tight martingale and a sharp snaffle. Ricky's face was red from exertion, although the lesson had barely begun.

Ivy and Emma were riding next to each other and chatting quietly while Kate walked around a little to the side of everybody with Prince. She kept beating the persistent flies away with a long branch that she'd broken from a bush outside the stable, and every time Kate and Prince came close to Burly, Burly immediately stretched his neck to try to grab a couple of yummy leaves. Mia was a little embarrassed at what her hungry horse was doing, but only she and Kate seemed to notice his pranks, and Kate just smiled cheerfully and pulled the branch away every time so that Burly couldn't reach it.

Mia looked up at the sky. It had stopped raining, but the clouds were still thick and dark. When the rain stopped earlier the air had felt fresh and nice, but now it was getting oppressive again and Mia noticed Burly's neck was already slick with sweat, although they were only walking at a leisurely pace.

The lesson was soon in full swing. Greta worked them hard, and Mia was soon as soaked with sweat as her horse. They did transitions, halts, tempo changes and circle tracks. Greta seemed to be able to watch them all simultaneously, and Mia discovered that it was impossible to relax for even one second.

At the end, they got to jump a couple of obstacles. Mia's legs were wobbly and she hardly had the energy to drive her horse forward, but Burly was good-natured and jumped anyway.

"Push him more," Greta said. "He needs more energy."

Mia rode a circle track and went for the two obstacles again. She drove and drove, but Burly didn't want to jump. He probably thought that he'd done his day's work. Mia aided with her legs and clicked her tongue furiously, although her legs were tired and her mouth dry.

Burly jumped the first obstacle almost from a standstill, and Mia lost her balance. She regained it in a moment, but when she turned Burly to the second obstacle nothing helped. He just walked slower and slower with every stride. Mia clicked and drove, and finally rapped Burly behind the girth with her crop, but that only made him buck, which caused her to lose her balance again.

When he finally stopped, right in front of the obstacle, Mia was totally helpless. She slowly slid from the saddle and landed on the ground.

In a daze, Mia lay completely still, staring up at the gray clouds and thinking, "This isn't happening to me."

She heard Kate call out encouragingly from far off, but she was sure the others were laughing at her.

"Are you all right?"

Greta hurried up to Mia. She sounded worried, probably because Mia hadn't gotten up at once but was still lying on her back, so Mia drew a deep breath and sat up.

"I think so," she answered, still dazed. "Where's Burly?"

Burly immediately realized that this was his chance. He was already grazing calmly at the edge of the ring, where there was thick green grass.

"I'll get him," Greta offered. "Can you ride more?"

"Of course!" Mia had said, getting to her feet. "But I'd better try to catch Burly myself. He doesn't always want to…"

But it was too late. Greta was walking up to Burly with one hand held forward, as if she was offering him a treat. Burly gave her an interested look from under his bangs. He then turned and trotted the other way. Mia tried to catch the swinging reins when he passed her, but Burly easily jumped to the side and ran to the other end of the ring, where there was more grass.

"Burly!" Mia roared, but he didn't care one bit. He felt that he had earned a break, and this was the time for it. To no avail, Mia tried to catch him a few more times, while the others considerately walked around to the far end of the ring.

"I need a bucket of oats," Mia had said to Greta. "I'll get one in the stable."

She ran all the way to the stable, uttering a lot of words

31

that her parents wouldn't have liked to hear about her hopeless horse. She was totally embarrassed and incredibly mad at her stubborn horse that wouldn't let himself be caught.

It was so typical of Burly to let her down today, the most important day of her life. Oh, she was so angry! She was never going to take him to something like this camp again, that was for sure.

Still, it was with a soft, tender voice that she called Burly's name again a while later, now with the bucket held high. The oats rattled invitingly at the bottom and Burly, who was probably starting to get bored with grass, decided to take the risk and examine the bucket more closely. He was soon caught and Mia mounted again. She was as angry as a hornet, and while the others finished their jumping and walked their horses to the stable, she rode up to the obstacles again.

It felt as if she suddenly got all her energy back, and the nervousness she had felt earlier was totally gone. Now she would show Burly and Greta the real score.

Burly noticed the change and pulled himself together, and when Mia took him toward the two obstacles again, he flew over them with inches to spare.

"See, he can do it if he wants to," Greta called when Mia pulled him up, her face red with exertion.

"Sure, when he *wants* to, then he can."

"And when *you* want to," Greta went on, patting Burly on his sweaty neck.

Mia looked at her with surprise. What did she mean?

"You were too easy on him before," Greta said kindly. "You have a strong, tough horse, and you have to be equally strong and tough in return. As soon as you got angry and pushed him hard, he jumped just fine. Now praise him and then take him back to the stable. There's a hose there, so you can hose him down."

Mia nodded and gave Burly extra rein. With long strides, he walked out of the riding ring. Mia patted his neck.

"You bad boy," she whispered. "Now we know what's what. From now on you won't decide a single thing, just so you know."

Burly nodded. Either he understood exactly what she had said, or he was just getting rid of some persistent flies. Anyway, he seemed quite content with himself after jumping those obstacles, and Mia had felt her confidence returning.

Mia yawned and turned over in bed. It had started raining again, and the sound of raindrops on the window was soothing. A moment later, she was sound asleep and she didn't wake up until Kate shook her and yelled something about "breakfast" in her ear.

CHAPTER 4

The next morning, Mia was tender everywhere after her fall. At breakfast, when Greta told them she was going to work with them in smaller groups for the morning session, Mia noted with relief that she and Linda would be riding last.

"Aren't you sore from yesterday?" Linda asked when they sat down together on the grass by the riding ring.

"You bet," Mia groaned, making a face, "but I can ride, and that's the most important thing. I'm not going to miss one second of this camp!"

Linda nodded.

"Me neither. I think I learned a lot yesterday. I've mostly been riding Graygirl in the woods, because Grandpa doesn't have a ring and I'm not allowed to ride in the pen."

"Where's Graygirl from?" Mia asked. Linda played a little with the grass where she was sitting.

"I don't know," she said. "Grandpa bought her from a horse trader a couple of months ago. She was dangerously thin and very nervous, but she must have had at least one good owner before, because she loves to be cared for. And she's the nicest horse in the world to ride."

"Her head is very beautiful," Mia said, watching the three horses and riders out in the ring. "Do you know what breed she is?"

"No idea," Linda said. "I think she has some Arab in her, and maybe Connemara or New Forest. But I'll probably never know. And it doesn't matter. I like her because she is who she is."

In the ring in front of them, Kate, Emma and Ivy were warming up their horses by trotting them across cavaletti poles on the ground. Greta was busy building three bounce obstacles.

Mia looked at the obstacles with interest. They were so close together that the horses had to jump them very quickly, and Mia knew what they were because it looked like the horses were bouncing over the obstacles.

Kate and Prince went first, and they quickly and easily slid across the three X's a few times and received praise from Greta. It was obvious they had done this before, and Mia was very surprised to see both horse and rider change so much. Kate, who usually seemed scatterbrained and reckless, was now determined and careful. And the sourpuss Prince looked like a new horse when he flew toward the obstacles, his ears pricked in a lovely gallop and his tail waving like a flag behind him.

Then it was Ivy and Samson's turn. Samson threw his head eagerly when he saw the obstacles, and Ivy tugged at his mouth for all she was worth, but she didn't stand a chance. Samson just ripped the reins out of her hands, rushed for the obstacles and threw himself at them. He managed the first one, but knocked down the other two, making the poles fly every which way.

It took a while, but Ivy finally managed to rein him in. Her face was red when she rode over to Greta, who had called for her.

"Have you been trotting cavaletti with him and just jumping low obstacles at a trot, as I suggested so many times this spring?" she asked. Ivy looked embarrassed.

"Well, a couple of times… We've had competitions almost every weekend, and I've had a lot to do in school, and…"

"So how well does he do in the competitions?" Greta asked, and Ivy immediately looked happier.

"He always jumps and he's fast, so we usually get good results. This last time, we actually won Easy A and were third in the middle difficulty. There were only five horses, but still…"

Mia could feel her stomach fall. Middle difficulty! She would be the happiest girl in the world if she and Burly could get a rosette in Easy C sometime in the far future.

"There are cavaletti poles over there," Greta said to Ivy and pointed to the other end of the riding ring. "I want you to trot them at an easy tempo while Emma jumps the bounce obstacles. And Samson is to trot, not gallop."

"Cavaletti? But… I mean, he knows how to jump. Can't we try again?" she asked, but Greta shook her head.

"Trot the poles first. Come on now, Emma. Get Jolly up to speed, so you can jump as soon as I've rebuilt the obstacles."

Ivy looked annoyed when she trotted off, and Emma gave her a sympathetic look. Then she started trotting around on Jolly Gray Delight, a beautiful pony who was fourteen years old and completely white. The pony looked sweet, and Emma rode with very long reins and didn't seem to be driving her at all.

"Here you go!" Greta called, and Emma aimed for the bounce obstacles.

Her pony took off at a gallop on her own and jumped easily and without problems.

"Shorten your reins and do it again," Greta ordered.

Emma did something with her reins, but Mia could see that they were almost as loose now as they were before when she turned toward the obstacles again. It seemed as if Jolly was going to jump anyway, but right before the obstacles, she veered off to the right and passed the jumps on the side. It looked easy and elegant and Emma didn't even lose her balance. A few yards further off, Jolly went into a trot. Emma rode a circle and came back to Greta with an embarrassed smile on her face.

"You have to hold her with your leg aids," Greta said. "Be more firm and shorten your reins even more. Right now, she's just running off with you and doing as she pleases."

Jolly stretched her head out to Greta and sniffed her with ears pricked. Greta laughed and patted her muzzle.

"She does that when she wants sugar," Emma said. "She always gets a lump of sugar when I jump her at home. By the way, how short do you want my reins to be? I've already shortened them a lot!"

Then Mia didn't hear what she said, because at that moment, Ricky came riding on Mistral. Just as they rode into the ring, the sun broke through the gray clouds and seemed to shine just for Mistral. He danced on the track. His golden coat was shining and his muscles played beneath his thin skin. He looked like liquid gold! Mia's arms were covered with goose bumps. Mistral was the most beautiful horse she had ever seen.

She followed Ricky and Mistral with her eyes when they started trotting around at the other end of the ring, so as not to disturb the jumpers, and she couldn't help wishing that Burly were just a little like Mistral. Of course the thought immediately made her feel guilty. Her lovely, beautiful horse! Who cared that he was a cute, round Fjord horse instead of one of those hot-blooded types that loved to prance around all the time. Because prancing around was exactly what Mistral was doing.

Ricky had had problems with his hot-blooded pony yesterday, and Mistral was no calmer today. On the contrary, he threw his head, jumped around and shied at everything. Mia admired Ricky, who was able to keep Mistral under control anyway. Even Samson looked like a calm, plodding riding school horse next to the cream-colored one.

"Let's prepare our horses," Linda said and elbowed Mia a little.

Mia nodded. Yes, it was time.

She looked at the riding ring one last time before she rose, moaning quietly, and followed Linda to the stable. Inside, everything was calm and quiet. Burly and Graygirl were standing half asleep, but Burly raised his head, pricked his ears and neighed softly when he saw Mia. She gave him a quick hug before starting to brush him. She still had pangs of bad conscience for wishing, just for a moment, that he was another horse, but Burly just nudged her gently and begged for a treat by scraping his fore-hoof on the stable floor.

A moment later, they heard hooves clip-clopping outside the stable, and Kate and Emma came riding in. Mia heard them talking as they dismounted and quickly went to the tack room to get her things. If those two were back, she and Linda needed to hurry.

"Are we on soon?" Linda asked as soon as Kate came into the passageway with Prince.

Kate smiled and shook her head.

"No, don't worry, but ride over there and have a look, 'cause it's all pretty interesting. Mistral has already broken three poles!"

"You're kidding!" Linda exclaimed, but Kate shook her head.

"Oh, no. He's a real bad boy. Worse than Prince, actually!"

"He's crazy," said Emma who had also come in, "but Ricky rides him beautifully, I must say."

"A minute ago, you thought it was his cute smile that was so beautiful," Kate teased her, leading Prince to his stall next to Burly.

"Hah," said Emma, letting go of Jolly's reins.

The mare went into her stall herself while Emma took her helmet off and raked her fingers through her sweaty, blonde bangs, pushing them away from her forehead.

But Emma shouldn't have let go of Jolly. The mare was very sweaty after the lesson, and before Emma could stop her, she folded her legs and rolled in the dry sawdust on the stall floor.

"No, Jolly! Get up! Stupid horse!" Emma shouted, running into the stall.

She clicked her lips and kept yelling at Jolly, and finally managed to get the horse to stand up before she rolled over with her saddle on.

"Why don't you just lead her into the stall?" Kate asked softly. "That seems easier."

"Jolly *always* walks into the stall herself," Emma said angrily. "I don't understand why she's acting so strange here! It has to be because it's a new stable."

"I think it's because she's sweaty and itching. Most horses like to scratch themselves then," Linda said kindly.

Emma gave her an angry look.

"I've had my horse much longer than you, actually, and I certainly know what my horse does and why!"

Linda looked squashed and Mia felt sorry for her. Emma shouldn't have attacked Linda like that. They were all here to learn things they didn't know, and Emma certainly wasn't the best rider in the group. Mia had learned that when she saw Emma riding earlier.

"Anyway, Prince rolls, too," Emma said to Kate, who was on her way to the tack room.

"Sure, but I usually take his saddle and bridle off first," Kate smiled. "Come on, let's go watch the jumping. How many poles do you think Mistral has destroyed by now? Four, or maybe seven?"

"I think you ought to stop making jokes about him!" Emma hissed from inside Jolly's stall. "Just because you have a nice, sweet-tempered horse…"

Mia didn't hear the end of the sentence. She had already led Burly out in the yard. She didn't want to hear, either. She and Burly were more important now. Her stomach fluttered when she tightened the girth and mounted.

CHAPTER 5

In the ring, Ricky and Ivy were jumping their horses. Greta had kept only one of the bounce obstacles and put three cavaletti poles in front of it on the ground. The idea was that the horses would trot over the cavalettis and then jump the little X in rhythm without rushing.

Samson already seemed to have understood what she wanted. He was moving in a much more relaxed way now, trotting over the poles, taking one gallop stride and easily jumping the X.

"Good, Ivy," Greta praised. "That's enough for the two of you today. You can try now, Ricky."

Ricky immediately went for the obstacle and Mistral threw himself into a quick gallop. He almost fell when he tripped on the cavaletti poles, but he managed to straighten things out and made a long, flat jump over the little X. Ricky tugged and tore at his mouth and Mia ached inside when she saw Mistral show the whites of his eyes and toss his head back and forth to escape the bit. Ricky swore at his horse, and then finally, at long last, he managed to stop Mistral, far away at the other end of the ring.

"Calm down," Greta called to them, "both of you!"

"Gosh, what a crazy horse," Ivy said to Linda and Mia when they met at the gate. "I can't understand how Ricky manages him. But then he's a terrific rider."

But Mia didn't think that Ricky was a good rider at all. Instead, she wanted to defend Mistral, and felt that it wasn't the horse's fault when everything went wrong. He was afraid; you could see that from far away, Mia thought. If he had been her horse, instead of punishing him she would have tried to calm him down by patting him, talking to him and trying to avoid jerking at the reins all the time.

But she didn't mention her opinion to Ivy, who seemed to think that Ricky was doing the only right thing. Instead Mia just nodded, as if in agreement, and then grumbled at her own cowardice for several minutes as she warmed up Burly. It was hard to concentrate, since Mistral came galloping around the track at full speed from time to time. But he calmed down after a while, when he got to trot the cavalettis again and then trot-jump the X.

Mia tried to forget everything else and just think about Burly. He was his usual quiet self, but Mia still managed to get him up to speed. When she looked toward the obstacle again a little while later, she could see Ricky walking around Greta on Mistral, talking agitatedly to her. Mia couldn't hear what they said, but she understood that it was about Mistral, since his name was mentioned several times.

When it was finally Mia's and Linda's turn to jump, Ricky had disappeared into the stable, and Mia realized with relief that she and Linda were alone in the ring. Now she didn't have to feel like she was being stared at, the way she did yesterday, and suddenly everything was a thousand times easier. With firm aids, she turned Burly toward the bounce obstacles and he jumped as if he'd been doing them all his life.

"Now do the bounces one more time, and then you can turn left and jump that oxer over there," Greta said, and Mia gave her a surprised look.

Nobody else had jumped anything but the bounces, so why was she? But she didn't bother to ask. Instead she did as Greta told her, and Burly seemed to think it was wonderful fun. He really got into it and flew across the oxer in a long, high jump that made Mia slide a little backwards. She almost tore at his mouth, but then she remembered to open her hand and let the rein slide between her fingers.

She jumped a couple of times more before Greta thought that it was enough. Greta had lots of praise for both Mia and Burly. Mia felt very embarrassed, and most of all wanted to jump down from Burly and give him a big hug, but she dismounted discreetly a minute later while Linda was jumping, loosened the girth and let Burly graze.

Burly affectionately rubbed his head against her. He was sweaty and his bridle was itching. He also made sure that she got a few really nice grass stains on her best shirt, but who cared. Today Mia would forgive him anything.

Mia looked at Linda and Graygirl. Graygirl was hardly broken in at jumping, so she also got to do the exercise with trotting poles first, and then the X.

At first Graygirl didn't seem to understand what Linda and Greta meant at all, but she did her best and soon got the hang of it. After a couple of really nice jumps she was done, and the girls kept each other company back to the stable.

There was Ricky, talking to Ivy and Emma. He seemed calmer now, but talked loudly about how badly behaved and rowdy Mistral had been and how hard he had worked with his horse all winter. Ivy and Emma listened with interest, and now and then Ivy made some comment about how she had trained Samson. Emma didn't say a word. She looked at Ricky with admiration and smiled slightly to herself, pushing her bangs away from her forehead every now and then.

Mia led Burly into his stall and removed his saddle. Burly immediately put his muzzle down into the feeder to find something edible, and sadly noticed that it was empty. Luckily, he found a couple of pieces of hay that he'd missed earlier.

"So, are you going to try a new bit on him?" Ivy asked Ricky in the passageway, and Mia pricked her ears.

"Well, I guess I'll have to, but I can't understand how Greta thinks I'm going to be able to control him with an ordinary snaffle. But we can always try."

Mia patted Burly's sweaty neck and went out into the passageway with his saddle and bridle.

"I don't think Greta really understands that Mistral is a rough and tough horse that needs his rider to be equally rough," Ricky said when Mia passed by.

Mia felt anger boiling up inside her and once again she wanted to defend Mistral, but didn't say anything. Instead, she just kept going, eyes stiffly forward and jaw tense.

Before she even opened the door to the tack room she started regretting that she hadn't said anything, but what would she have said? They would hardly listen to her anyway. She was just a rookie, compared to Ivy and Ricky who had been in lots of competitions. They would have just laughed at her.

In the tack room, Kate was removing the saddle pad from Prince's saddle. She looked up and smiled when Mia came in.

"What are you doing?" Mia asked in surprise.

"The pad is soaked with sweat, so I'm hanging it in the sun. It'll be dry before afternoon. Are you letting Burly out?"

"Yes, if there's a good pen."

"Would you dare let him go with Prince? He can't go by himself, so it would be really nice of you," Kate said. She looked at Mia, who smiled.

"Sure. If he's well behaved, why not? I noticed you did well. You made it look so easy, when you just flew over the obstacles."

"Oh," Kate said, a little embarrassed. "Prince is so good. I just tag along and he does all the work. But certain other people seem to think they're doing the jumping and not their horses," she added ironically, nodding toward the stable.

"I like Ricky even less now," she went on. "I've stopped thinking of him as a goody-two-shoes who goes to Sunday School, but I'm starting to think he'll need to, the way he treats his poor horse."

"Do you feel sorry for Mistral, too?" Mia asked, and Kate nodded.

"Sure. He looks terrified, the poor thing…"

Kate was suddenly quiet, since the door opened and Linda walked in. She panted as she hung up her saddle and rubbed sweat from her forehead.

"If I don't get anything to drink soon I'm going to faint," she moaned, walking into the little bathroom next to the tack room.

There were plastic cups in there and Linda filled one from the tap and drank in big gulps. Then she sighed deeply.

47

"I have never tasted better water," she said, smiling at the two girls. "I thought I'd faint in the heat out there. At home, I never ride in the middle of the day, but only early in the morning or late at night."

"Early in the morning? You have to be crazy! You could be sleeping instead," Kate said cheerily. "Come on now, let's go ask Greta if she has a pen for our horses. I bet you'd like to let Graygirl out, too?"

"Yes, absolutely," Linda exclaimed. "I was just going to ask what you were going to do. Greta is out in the stable now, talking to the others. Come on, let's hurry."

A few minutes later, the horses were out grazing in the pens. Prince and Burly had immediately become friends, while Graygirl and Jolly were walking in the next pen. Graygirl started grazing as if she had never seen food before, while Jolly trotted back and forth excitedly, trying to catch the eye of the geldings, although she soon grew tired of that game and started eating too.

Samson and Mistral were in a third pen. At first, Ivy wasn't sure she wanted to let Samson out at all.

"He's not used to grazing freely," she said to Greta, knitting her eyebrows. "I don't want him to get fat."

"That pen over there is one of the ones I use in the winter," Greta said calmly. "There are mostly weeds there and almost nothing to eat. I think you can let him graze there without worrying."

Ivy looked at her watch.

"Okay, I'll let him graze for one hour, but not one minute more than that."

Mia stood leaning against the wooden fence and looking at Burly for a long time. She was in a good mood and smiled to herself, chewing on a blade of grass. Jumping had gone better than she had hoped, and she was slowly but surely beginning to feel at home at Edinburgh. That feeling of being an outsider was slowly fading away, and she happily decided to call her parents and tell them everything.

CHAPTER 6

"Eek! No, help! Get it away from me!"

A scream that could have awakened the dead made Mia drowsily sit up in bed. Kate was standing in the door, screaming, with her comforter wrapped around her. She pointed a chubby finger at the window, where a poor insect was buzzing around, trying to find its way out.

"A wasp! Get it out of here," Kate moaned in despair. "I'm scared to death of wasps."

"It's not a wasp, it's a bee," Mia said calmly. She

opened the window wide, allowing the poor little bee to return to freedom. "Bees are nice."

"Ugh," Kate said, carefully walking back to her bed.

She looked suspiciously at the window and made a face.

"I don't care what you call it, 'cause everything with a striped abdomen that stings and buzzes scares the living daylights out of me."

"Easy now," Mia said, giggling. "It's gone. And anyway, it was a very small bee."

"Small!?" Kate exclaimed in horror. "It was at least two yards wide, from eye to eye!"

The two girls laughed and a while later they walked together downstairs to the kitchen. Outside, the sun was shining from a clear blue sky and a warm breeze was wafting through the open window. Greta was setting the table for breakfast, and Mia and Kate helped her.

"What are we doing today?" Kate asked, and Greta looked out through the window.

"I thought about going on a trail ride to a lake a few miles away, and taking hot dogs to grill. If you want to, that is."

"Of course we want to!" Kate yelled. "That sounds great!"

"What sounds great?" Ivy asked, coming into the kitchen. "Are we show jumping today?"

"No, we're going on a long trail ride," Mia said. "Isn't that great?"

Ivy's brow furrowed and she looked surprised.

"But this is an educational camp. I thought…"

"Stop it, will you," Kate said, softly elbowing her. "Samson can use a break, and a chance to see something other than obstacles now and then. The weather's wonderful."

Ivy still looked disappointed, but when Emma and Ricky said they thought that the idea of going for a long ride and a swim was great she didn't say any more.

Now Linda was the only one missing. Mia was just about to go get her when she scrambled into the kitchen, with her hair on end and eyes sleepy.

"I overslept," she yawned. "I think my alarm clock is broken."

"No, it's not," Ivy hissed in irritation. "I heard it through the wall ages ago. It woke *me* up! And I wanted to sleep a little longer today."

"Hmm, I think Ivy got out on the wrong side of the bed this morning," Kate teased. "Maybe you should go back to bed, and then get out on the right side, whichever that might be…"

Ivy snorted angrily but didn't say anything. A minute later, they were all eating breakfast while Greta packed their lunch in a big basket. Nick would drive everything to the lake in the car, so they wouldn't have to bring all the stuff on the horses.

About an hour later, everybody was ready to go. Mia looked around the yard. She, Linda and Kate were standing together. Kate had already mounted Prince, who looked as sour as usual. Graygirl, on the other hand, seemed very curious about what was happening. She looked around with interest, ears pricked, while Burly mostly wanted to chow down on a big tuft of dandelions growing close to the stable wall that he'd just discovered.

Mia tightened the girth while she tried to stop Burly from eating. She was just about to mount him when Ivy led Samson out through the other stable door, a little further down.

Ivy still seemed to be in a bad mood and Mia thought that she probably still wanted to do some ring exercises, but Mia felt that it would be nice to take a break from riding the course today. The night before, they had had a long dressage lesson, and they had all been very tired afterwards. Mia could feel all that hard work today – when she mounted she had aches and pains in every part of her body.

Not that she minded. Mia thought that she had learned a lot, and Burly had started walking very well. Greta had given her lots of good advice about how to take him in hand and work in the right way.

Mia hoped that she would be able to remember at least half of the advice Greta had given her. She wanted to be able to show Tessa how nicely Burly could walk.

Mia looked over at Ivy again. Samson stomped around when Ivy wanted to mount, and Ivy hopped with one foot in the stirrup and the other on the ground. The dark gray gelding must have sensed that Ivy was in a bad mood. She angrily yelled at him to stand still.

"I wonder why Ivy is in such a bad mood," Linda said quietly to Mia, nodding at Samson.

"I can tell you," Kate whispered conspiratorially at Linda and Mia. "She's jealous. Her best friend just stole the only guy at the camp right out from under her nose. Didn't you see those two lovebirds Emma and Ricky cooing on the sofa in front of the TV last night? Ivy doesn't like that. She's used to getting all the boys."

Kate smiled and fell silent, throwing a meaningful look at Emma and Ricky. Mia looked over as well. Emma's and Ricky's horses were standing very close to each other and Emma kept turning her head, smiling and giving Ricky amorous glances. Ricky mostly seemed embarrassed.

Mia couldn't help feeing a little jealous, not because she liked Ricky, but because Emma had somebody who liked her. Mia was way too shy to even think that somebody might be interested in her.

Her thoughts were interrupted when Ivy rode over to them on Samson.

"He's so stupid today," she growled, patting Samson on his neck. It seemed more like she was slapping him, Mia thought.

"And you're in a very bad mood," Kate smiled. "I think he can sense it and he's making fun of you. Samson is clever and strong, you know."

"Oh, cut it out," Ivy growled. "Anyway, I don't feel like trail riding at all. I want to jump. That's why we're here, isn't it? I can ride out in the woods at home any time I want to."

"Actually, it's good to let your horse do different things," Linda suddenly said. Ivy gave her a surprised look. That shy little Linda would dare say something like that to her, of all people, must have been quite a surprise.

"Competition horses have to see more than the track every once in a while," Linda went on. "My grandfather always trains his trotters on the forest roads at home, and both of them have won several competitions this year."

"Oh," Ivy said, disinterestedly shrugging her shoulders. "But Samson likes to walk the course and he gets so troublesome out in the woods. He always has to walk first, and he won't stop fussing."

She straightened her helmet, and Mia turned to look at Greta and her jumper Martinique, who had just come out of the stable. Martinique was about 68 inches and dark brown with a stripe. Although Martinique was big, Greta mounted him easily, and they were finally ready to go.

"Ride single file, and keep about one horse length between the horses, so they can't kick each other," Greta said. "Ricky, you follow me with Mistral, so he only has one horse in front of him. I think that will keep him calm."

Emma quickly rode Jolly up behind Mistral, and then Ivy, Kate, Linda and finally Mia followed. Burly snorted and threw his head back and forth to get rid of some flies. He felt energetic and tense and Mia suspected that he would go pretty fast if they galloped later.

There was great riding terrain around the farm, and

both horses and humans enjoyed trotting along the soft, winding paths.

After a while, they came onto a somewhat bigger forest road and Greta told them to gallop. Burly eagerly snorted and suddenly bucked with pure happiness. Mia just laughed at him. She could tell that he knew what was coming.

In front of them everything seemed to be going smoothly, even at a gallop. Mistral was just behind Martinique, and didn't try to overtake him, although Mia could hear Mistral snorting over and over again, and she could see Ricky sawing repeatedly at his mouth.

But Ricky wasn't the first to run into problems. It was Samson who suddenly threw himself to one side and tried to pass everybody. Ivy yelled something, Greta pulled Martinique up and everybody slowed to trot and then a walk. Samson slowed down too, but now Ivy was angry for real.

"I can't keep Samson this far back in the line," she snorted at Emma who was riding in front of her. "I have to ride further up. Move over, Emma."

"But Jolly's on edge too," Emma tried to protest, although the mare had walked calmly and peacefully, as she always did.

"Move it! That old camel doesn't move an inch if she doesn't have to," Ivy said angrily. "C'mon, Emma."

"But…" Emma began, but by then it was already too late. Ivy had passed her with Samson, and after Greta had agreed to the new line-up they moved on.

"Let's trot now," Greta said. "We'll soon come to a hard gravel road where we have to walk."

The gravel road soon appeared and then they walked for a couple of miles. The sun relentlessly fried them from the clear blue sky and the heat was unbearable. All the horses walked on long reins, and even Mistral and Samson seemed to have calmed down.

Burly kept shaking his head and whipping his long tail. The flies were irritating, and Mia succeeded in killing several horseflies that landed on his neck and behind the saddle to bite him. Mia finally followed Kate's example, breaking off a long branch from a bush and waving it around.

Burly seemed satisfied with her help with the flies, but of course he couldn't stop trying to grab a little of the delicious green that kept passing him when Mia waved the branch over his head. He gave up when Mia just laughed at him and his pranks.

"Are we staying on this road for long?" Ivy asked. Greta shook her head.

"We'll be back in the forest soon."

Ivy took her helmet off and raked her hand through her sweaty hair. Greta, who was just turning around to say something to Ricky, saw this and immediately pulled Martinique up.

"Put your helmet on at once. You're not allowed to ride without a helmet. You know that."

"So what?" Ivy said. "I'm disintegrating from the heat. What's the danger now, when we're just walking?"

"Either put the helmet on or dismount and walk," Greta said angrily. "Come on, just do it."

Ivy muttered something that Mia couldn't hear, but at least she put the helmet on and did up the chinstrap.

Ricky turned and said something to her and Ivy suddenly laughed in what sounded like satisfaction. She rode up alongside Ricky and then they sat talking while Emma had to ride behind on Jolly.

Kate turned to Mia, smiled and shook her head. Mia knew exactly what she meant. Now it seemed to be Ivy's turn to try to attract Ricky's interest.

A little later, they turned onto a logging road and Greta called for them to trot again. The horses were happy to move their legs and leave the flies and the hot gravel behind. The logging road wound all through the big forest and Mia truly enjoyed herself.

Soon, Greta started galloping, and this time it worked better for everybody. Burly snorted and was hard on the bit, but Mia talked soothingly to him and he knew that it was useless trying to get the upper hand over the stubborn human he had in the saddle, so he obediently stayed at the back of the line.

After a while, the forest became less dense and the seven riders and their horses could see blue water ahead. Greta slowed to a walk again and they all gave their horses long reins.

The road ended at a beautiful little swimming cove

where Nick and Greta's big red car was parked. Nick was preparing lunch and the smell of grilled meat met them. Mia suddenly realized how hungry she was, and when she looked at her watch she noticed it was after one o'clock. They had been in the saddle for two and a half hours, and it was wonderful to dismount.

"My legs!" Kate moaned when she slowly slid down from Prince's back. "I'm dying, I'm sure! My body wasn't built for this much exercise."

"Ha ha! Serves you right. I said we should have stayed home and jumped instead," Ivy said cheerfully, no longer sounding anything like the sourpuss she had been earlier in the morning. Mia guessed that Ricky was the cause of the change. He now seemed to be talking only to Ivy, while Emma was standing on the sidelines, looking sad.

Mia went up to Nick, who had brought head collars and lead reins for the horses. The idea was to tie the horses to trees, but Ivy objected.

"Samson can't stand tied up. You know that," she said to Nick, as if everything was his fault.

"Okay, then you'll have to stand and hold him," Nick answered cheerfully.

"Did you bring a bucket for Mistral to drink from?" Ricky said. Nick gave him a surprised look.

"There's a whole lake over there, with ordinary water in it."

Ricky blushed and Mia almost felt sorry for him, but then, he'd asked an unusually stupid question, she thought as she led Burly down to the water and let him drink. He was sweaty under the saddle and Mia tried to wash him as well as she could. Burly seemed to enjoy this and suddenly started kicking his foreleg, splashing water everywhere.

"Cut it out," yelled Emma who happened to be close. "I'm getting totally wet! Get your stupid horse out of here!"

"Sorry," Mia giggled. "We didn't mean to."

Still laughing, she led Burly up on the shore, but they didn't get far before Burly started scraping his hoof in the sand again. Mia didn't know what was happening and at first she wanted to stop him, but when she saw how he enjoyed lying down in the sand and rolling over, she was glad she hadn't.

"You're out of your mind," Ivy yelled. "Are you going to let him keep rolling? He'll never be clean again!"

"He enjoys it," Mia called back. "And aren't we going to swim with the horses after we've eaten?"

She gave Greta a questioning look and Greta nodded.

"Sure, if you want to you can. But hurry up now, the food's ready."

"Yes, we're having grilled horsemeat," Nick joked and Kate made a face at him.

"So, did you sacrifice the slowest trotter on the farm?" she asked. Nick laughed.

"You bet," he said, waving a fork in the air. "Rest assured, Kate, if Prince doesn't point his ears forward soon, he'll be the next victim!"

"Shame on you for saying things like that about my lovely horse," Kate said, hugging Prince, who actually pricked his ears and looked at Nick, who still held his fork high.

Prince did not want to be grilled; that much seemed clear.

CHAPTER 7

After lunch, everybody was so tired that they just lay around relaxing. The horses were tied to trees, half asleep. They were tired after the long haul and also full of food, since Nick had brought hay for them. Even Samson had agreed to be tied up once food was within reach.

The only horse still awake seemed to be Burly, Mia thought as she lay looking at her horse. He had finished his hay long ago, yet he was now vacuuming the ground around his tree with his muzzle, as far as the lead rein allowed. If it was up to Burly, there wouldn't be one edible blade of grass left.

After their siesta, the riders went for a swim with the horses. The little cove was sandy, and the horses seemed to enjoy walking into the shallow water. Mia surprised everybody when she took Burly farther and farther away from the beach until finally, when the water was deep enough, she slid off him and swam quite a distance alongside her horse.

"That was so brave," Emma said, looking wide-eyed at her when she came back. "I would never dare try anything like that."

"If I swam out with Prince like that, he would probably drown me," Kate said with a smile. "But it sure does look like fun."

"I'd like to try too," Linda said. "How do you do it?"

Mia and Burly followed Linda and Graygirl out into the water, but Graygirl didn't like it when the water got deeper. She refused to go any further, so they had to head back to the beach again.

Ricky and Mistral didn't swim at all. Mistral refused to go into the water and finally Nick had to find a bucket and get some water for Mistral to drink. Ricky didn't get mad at his horse at all, Mia noted. He talked calmly to him, trying to encourage him, but to no avail. Mistral just did not want to swim.

A few hours later, it was time to pack up and ride home again. Everybody was panting and moaning when they got up on their horses again. Their muscles and behinds were sore from the long ride in the morning, but after they had ridden for a while everything loosened up and felt better.

They took another route home, following a narrow, winding path through scrubby woods and along a big tree-cleared logging area. All around them were cascades of crimson-red wild roses, but their beauty made little impression on Mia. She shuddered when she saw the clear-cut land, thinking that it was like a big wound on nature.

The horses were irritated and their tails whipped around. The horseflies were aggressive, and they didn't even ease up once the horses all went into a trot when the path widened and became less stony.

Now they were back in the woods and there was a smell of sun-warmed pine needles, summer and horses. The sunbeams filtered through the branches of the pines and the horses' hooves thudded dully on the needle-covered path.

It was all wonderful, but Mia felt too tired to care. Her legs and behind ached, and when Greta finally slowed to a walk she was as grateful as the others to relax for a while.

A little later, Greta stopped Martinique in a small clearing. The six pony riders gathered around her.

"Now, we have two roads to choose from, one short and one longer. I want to go the shorter route, since I think we're all pretty tired. But there is one problem. We'll have to cross a wooden bridge. Does anybody know if your horse is scared of bridges?"

Nobody said anything.

"So can we go that way?" Greta said, looking at them. "It's a dependable bridge, broad and easy to ride across."

"I want to go home," Kate said with feeling. "Let's go the shortest possible route, thank you."

"Yes, me too," Emma said. "I'll be too tired to sit up in a while."

Greta nodded.

"Okay, everybody. Then we go that way."

She turned onto a new logging road and everybody followed her in a neat row. Even the two troublemakers, Mistral and Samson, were a lot calmer now and walked peacefully on long reins alongside each other.

After a little while, Greta turned around in her saddle.

"Here's the bridge. Keep riding, shorten your reins, give leg aids, and make sure your horse follows right behind the one before it."

It was a wide wooden bridge across an equally wide ditch and Mia guessed that it was built to carry heavy machinery. Martinique crossed it without hesitating. He had no doubt crossed it before and didn't seem to mind that his hooves echoed when he went across.

Mistral, on the other hand, thought that the bridge was terribly scary. He stood stock-still and started reining back so quickly that first he bumped into Samson and then Jolly before Ricky could stop him.

Ricky clicked his tongue and tried to drive Mistral forward until he was red in the face, but it didn't help.

Mistral just stood there stomping the ground and reining back or turning in circles.

"Don't fuss with him," Greta said soothingly. "You others, ride across, and I'm sure he'll follow."

Emma rode up onto the bridge with Jolly, who walked obediently although her face looked somewhat suspicious. When Samson saw his stable friend disappear he bravely threw himself after her and Kate took the opportunity to follow with Prince, who suddenly found himself on the other side without really knowing how it had happened.

Linda dismounted from Graygirl, who looked totally scared when Linda asked her to come along across the bridge. With short, mincing steps and wide nostrils, she sneaked across on Linda's heels. Linda kept patting and praising her the whole time.

Now only Mia and Ricky were left. Mia looked at Ricky. She knew that Burly would cross.

"Do you want to go after me?" she asked. Ricky nodded.

Mistral was completely tense now. He rolled his eyes and his neck was sweaty. Ricky rode up until he was just behind Burly. Then he mumbled to Mia to hurry. He looked tense too, and tired, and for a moment Mia almost felt sorry for him.

Mia clicked at Burly, who safely and calmly walked out on the bridge without worrying at all. "We have one of these at home too," he seemed to be saying, and Mia wondered if horses could think like that. They actually did have a wooden bridge at home, which crossed a ditch between two fields, and she often rode that way when she was out galloping on her dad's fields in the fall.

Mia calmly rode over on Burly, but behind her she could hear Mistral's snorting and Ricky's voice. Ricky tried to talk soothingly and persuasively, but his tense voice revealed that he was anything but calm inside. As soon as he tried to get Mistral up on the bridge, the gelding shied back or threw himself to the side and turned around. Mistral had no intention of crossing this terrible bridge; that much was clear.

When Ricky still tried to force him, he started rearing up, and Ricky finally stopped bothering him. Instead, he dismounted and tried to lure Mistral across with a few dusty sugar cubes that he had in his pocket, but Mistral wasn't that easily fooled. He just threw his head back and forth and kept stomping in place without moving any closer to the bridge.

"Do you need help?" Greta asked. Her voice sounded worried.

"I can manage," Ricky hissed back.

Now he seemed to have lost his patience. He tugged angrily at Mistral's mouth and hit him with his crop, scolding his horse, but of course this didn't help. Mistral just danced away, even more scared than before.

"Let me try," Greta said, riding Martinique back across the bridge, but Ricky had already remounted.

"He's going to cross!" he said tightly while Greta rode up to him on Martinique.

"Try to make him follow me now," she said soothingly. "Relax, Ricky. It's going to be okay."

"I'm just so darned tired of this horse," Ricky said, ramming his heels into Mistral's sides, making the gelding jump straight up and snort. "He's going to cross now."

But it didn't work out this time either. Martinique obediently padded back and forth across the wooden bridge several times, but Mistral just stepped around.

"Okay," Greta said after trying a couple of times more. "We'll have to take the other route. Cross the bridge again, everybody. The other road will take an hour longer, but it's useless to try to get Mistral over."

There was a disappointed "oh no!" from Ivy and Emma, and Mia wanted to join in. Having to ride for another hour when they were just a couple of miles from home! It felt almost impossible, but there was nothing else to do.

She sighed and turned Burly away from the bridge, but then she pulled him up and looked over at the other side.

Ricky had galloped some distance away on Mistral. Mia looked at him, eyebrows knotted. What was he going to do? Ride all the way home by himself?

"Move out of the way, I'm going to jump!" Ricky shouted at that very moment and accelerated toward the ditch.

"Stop! You can't do that," Greta called back, but it was too late. Ricky had already chosen the place where the ditch was narrowest, and now Mistral galloped that way at full speed. Ricky kept slamming his knees into Mistrals sides, hitting him with the crop and clicking for all he was worth.

Mia held her reins tightly and closed her eyes. Ricky must be out of his mind. Mistral would never be able to get across the wide, deep ditch. They would kill themselves!

"Stop it, you idiot! Just stop it!"

Mia heard Greta shouting as loudly as she could, but Ricky wasn't going to obey her. When Mia looked up she saw Mistral flying like a bird, high above the ditch. He landed with a heavy thud on the other side, and it was nothing short of a miracle that Ricky stayed in the saddle.

Mistral slowed almost immediately and Ricky trotted up to the others. He looked satisfied with himself and patted Mistral's neck, praised the gelding and proudly smiled at the others, who just sat staring at him, mouths agape.

"That was the worst thing you could have done," Greta scolded him, but Ricky didn't even seem to hear her.

He just looked proud and superior and pulled up Mistral, who looked totally washed out. The chestnut's head was hanging and sweat was running along his neck and shoulders.

"Oh, stop going on like that. We made it. I knew Mistral could make it," Ricky said nonchalantly.

"That's not what this is about. You're going to do what I tell you to do," Greta said angrily. "I'm responsible for you and your horse and for everybody else here. You could have caused a terrible accident."

Ricky sighed and then smiled superciliously again. It looked as if he thought Greta should have been praising him instead of scolding him.

Greta looked at them all.

"Now let's walk home," she said angrily. "If just one more thing happens, Ricky, you're out of this camp. Got it?"

"Yes," Ricky mumbled, actually looking slightly embarrassed.

"He's crazy," Linda whispered to Mia when they started walking homewards again.

Mia nodded. She agreed with Linda. Still, she couldn't help admiring Ricky just a little. Imagine daring to jump across a ditch that wide and deep. She would never in her life dare trying something like that. She would rather have taken the long way home, if it had been her horse that had refused.

"Samson is lame," Ivy called out at that moment, and everybody stopped short.

Ivy jumped down and felt his left foreleg.

"He's been limping for several paces. Look! He doesn't want to put any weight on it at all. And his tendon is all hot," Ivy said accusingly to Greta, who had ridden up to her.

Greta dismounted from Martinique and felt Samson's leg for a long time.

"This leg doesn't feel any warmer than the others at all," she said eventually. "Did you check the hoof?"

"No, how can I? I don't have a hoof pick here," Ivy said.

Greta searched her vest pockets and found a hoof pick. She picked up Samson's hoof and found a sharp stone that was wedged between the shoe and the frog. She held the stone up for everybody to see and then gave it to Ivy.

"Here's the problem, I think. Now trot him a little, and let's see."

Ivy ran back and forth on the forest road with Samson, who now looked fine.

"How far until we're home?" Ivy asked.

"About a mile and a half," Greta said. "Why?"

"I think I'll lead him home," Ivy said. "I don't want to take any chances with my horse. I still think his leg feels warm. I'm not convinced that the stone was the problem."

Greta nodded without protesting. She then mounted Martinique and took the lead again. Well, if Ivy wants to walk that badly, let her walk, Mia thought.

Ivy and Samson were last in line now, after Burly. Mia turned around and tried talking to Ivy, but Ivy just seemed to be in an even worse mood and hardly answered, so Mia gave up.

As soon as they were home Ivy quickly led Samson into his stall and took off his saddle, and before anybody else had even thought that far she took Samson to the water box and started running cool water over his leg.

"How is he?" Linda asked in a friendly voice as she passed by on her way to the tack room with saddle and bridle.

"We'll see," Ivy said ominously. "I hope he'll be okay tomorrow. He limped several times on the way home. If there's a problem with a tendon, I might have to keep him in the stable for a long time."

"Do you really think it's that bad?" Emma said, opening her big blue eyes wide.

71

Ivy shrugged.

"Maybe. I said all along that going on a long ride was a bad idea. If my horse is hurt, I'll ask for my money back. We're here to do exercises, not to fool around in the woods."

"Oh, cut it out," said Kate, who had heard Ivy's comments. "A horse has to be able to walk in the woods without going lame."

"That's easy for you to say," Ivy snorted and gave Kate an angry look, "but Samson happens to be a real competition pony, and you have to be careful with those."

"Well, Prince has won a couple of rosettes too in his career," Kate said. "He and my sister came in second in the national finals last year. Wasn't that when you and Samson didn't even make it to the B finals?" she went on, tossing her hair and walking into the tack room.

Just then Greta came in and everybody stopped talking. Greta gave Samson and Ivy a questioning look.

"Are you going to be done soon? I think the others would like to wash their horses, too."

Mia thought that Greta didn't seem to understand why Ivy was standing there for so long.

"I have to rinse his leg until the swelling goes down," Ivy said.

"Swelling?" Greta said in surprise. "What swelling? He was fine when I felt him."

"His left leg was swollen when I took his saddle off," Ivy persisted, turning the water off. "Feel for yourself!"

72

Greta went over and felt Samson's leg with her hand. The gelding gently sniffed her and pricked his ears. He liked to be the center of attention and gladly stood still while Greta carefully felt both forelegs.

"I can't feel any swelling at all," Greta said slowly after a while.

"Well then, it must have helped that I cooled his leg down quickly with water," Ivy sad, pulling at Samson's lead rein.

With her nose in the air, she led Samson to his stall, and everybody went back to their own work.

"That horse isn't lame at all," Kate said when she, Mia and Linda were returning to the house a little later. "The only thing that's hurt is Ivy's pride."

"She should be glad it wasn't anything worse than a stone in a hoof," Linda said.

"Yes, this is a lot of fuss over nothing," Mia said.

"Yes, to us," Kate said, "but Ivy didn't like the idea of the long ride to begin with. If she can make it seem that Samson was hurt because of it I guess she's achieved her goal: to prove that she was right all along! And then she can squash Greta and the rest of us flat."

"I don't understand how she even has the energy for all that," Linda said. "I'd like the shower first, by the way."

"You can forget about that," Mia said, laughing. "I saw Emma run up to the house like lightning earlier. I'm sure she's already in the shower, and I bet she's going to stay there for a while."

"By the way, why did Greta tell Ricky that this was his last chance?" Linda said. "He hasn't done anything stupid before, has he?"

Kate nodded.

"You might say he has. Nick discovered Ricky and Emma were out after curfew last night. Ivy told me while we were swimming."

Suddenly Mia felt very small and childish, and once again that feeling of jealousy swelled inside. Nobody ever asked her if she wanted to go anywhere after curfew. Not that she *wanted* to, but…

She just wanted to be like Ivy and Emma, sort of cool and sure of herself; somebody who knew how to get what they wanted, instead of always being the silent, boring girl who nobody saw or even noticed.

But it was no use even trying to be like that, Mia bitterly thought while they climbed the stairs to the second floor. She'd always be who she was, a shy coward with no confidence at all when it came to being cool or relating to boys…

Then Kate said something that immediately put Mia in a better mood. They were right at Kate's and Mia's door, and Kate leaned over and looked secretive.

"Do you know what I've got? Licorice whips!" she whispered, and Mia started giggling.

Kate sounded as if she was going to tell them the greatest secret in the world, and although they were all alone in the corridor, she glanced around suspiciously to see if anybody was listening.

"I actually have a hoard of licorice whips hidden away, exactly for situations like this, when we're starving and suffering. Sound good? I'm totally hungry," Kate whispered.

"Me, too," Linda and Mia said in unison, and then it was only a matter of minutes before Kate's secret hoard was disappearing.

CHAPTER 8

The beautiful weather continued, and the next morning Mia was awakened by a tractor roaring close to her window. She silently padded to the window and looked out.

The sky was clear blue without a single cloud, the sun was beating down and she knew Nick was going to start haying today. He had mentioned it last night, as they sat on the porch.

Mia thought of her dad, who had probably started harvesting. He usually tried to get the hay in around midsummer, when it was at its greenest and most nutritious and the weather was mostly good. Mia hoped that the heat would stay. There was nothing worse than sitting in the kitchen at home and watching rain coming down and destroying the newly mown hay.

At that moment, the alarm clock started rattling and Kate mumbled something, pulling her comforter over her head. Mia reached over and turned the alarm off. Kate was always very sleepy in the mornings, and Mia could hardly resist playing a prank on her. But she didn't have the time, since Kate had wakened on her own for a change, and was sitting up in her bed yawning widely.

"What are you doing?" Kate asked, looking curiously at Mia. "Morning calisthenics?"

"No, I just woke up before the alarm," Mia said, sitting down on her bed. "Come on. We have stable duty today."

"Oh, I forgot," Kate said, yawning again. "We'd better hurry, then."

The stable was nice and cool in spite of the heat outside. Burly neighed eagerly when he saw Mia and Kate. Kate was sure that he was saying, "Where's my breakfast?"

Every night, everybody put their horses' morning meals outside the stalls, so morning feeding was quick. Mia and Kate were finished by the time Ivy walked in.

Ivy still seemed to be in a bad mood and hardly said "hi" before walking in to Samson. Mia and Kate went over to her, and when they looked into the stall they saw Ivy crouching by Samson's foreleg and feeling it carefully.

"How is he?" Kate asked in a friendly voice. Ivy sighed sadly.

"A little better, but I'm not sure I dare ride. What if he goes really lame? I'd never forgive myself."

She patted Samson's neck and left the stall.

While they walked back to the house, where breakfast was waiting in the kitchen, Mia thought that Ivy was making a silly fuss over Samson's leg. Greta had found the stone in his hoof yesterday and, from what Mia had seen, he hadn't limped at all after she removed it.

Ivy seemed to be exaggerating, Mia thought as she sat down at her usual place at the table. Maybe it had something to do with Emma and Ricky. Mia thought about what Kate had said last night, that Ivy and Emma had been best friends for years. And now Emma didn't care about Ivy at all. She hardly even spoke to her friend! Emma only had eyes for Ricky, and…

Mia's train of thought was interrupted when Greta gave her the breadbasket. It was full of newly baked muffins that smelled wonderful.

"This morning we're doing some show jumping," Greta said cheerfully. "That's okay, isn't it, Ivy?"

"Well," Ivy said, sighing again, "Samson's leg still feels warm. I don't know if I can."

"Then it's a good thing the vet is coming today," Nick

said. He was standing by the kitchen sink, gulping down a cup of coffee. "I'll ask him to have a look at your horse too. See you in the stable at ten."

He nodded and disappeared through the door.

Ivy looked after him, mouth gaping.

"Are any of your horses ill?" Emma asked Greta when Nick had left and the door had closed behind him.

"Not at all," Greta said, "but we let the vet check all the mares with ultrasound now and then. That way we can tell at an early stage if a mare is carrying. If she isn't, we can try to impregnate her again."

"That sounds smart," Emma exclaimed. "I had no idea you could do that."

"Didn't you?" Kate said in surprise. "I thought everybody knew that. By the way, they check humans with ultrasound too. Before the twins were born, my sister and I got to go to the hospital and see them, and that was really exciting!"

After breakfast, everybody went to the stable. Burly was standing half asleep in one corner of his stall, but when he saw Mia he neighed and pricked his ears as usual.

Mia went in and patted him. Then she put her bucket inside the stall door and started brushing Burly's coat with long, even strokes.

Out in the passageway, she could hear Ricky and Greta discussing the use of different bits. Finally, she heard Ricky agree to try a thick, jointed snaffle for Mistral instead of the sharp bit he had now.

"But I bet he'll take off on me like crazy," Ricky said. Mia could hear metal rattling in the passageway.

"In that case, we'll make him stop," Greta said calmly. "Try it anyway. It might be that he's running because he's afraid his mouth will hurt. Some sensitive horses like a softer bit a lot better."

"His last owner rode him with this bit," Ricky said. "He said it was necessary. And my coach at home says I use my hands so softly that it's okay to use a sharp bit."

"Try anyway," Greta said persuasively. "It worked with Martinique."

Ricky and Greta went to change bits and Mia started scratching Burly's chest. He put his big head against her shoulder, and the more Mia scratched the heavier he got. It felt like at least a ton of Fjord horse was leaning against her.

"You'll have to move over now. I have to pick your hooves out," Mia said at last, softly pushing Burly away.

He looked reproachfully at her. "And I was having such a good time!" he seemed to say, before sighing deeply and starting to look for bits of hay that he might have missed during breakfast.

"Come on, we're building the course," Kate called as she entered the stable.

Mia, Ricky, Linda and Emma walked up to Kate, who was holding a sheet of paper in her hand.

"This is the plan. Greta just gave it to me," Kate explained, holding up the paper for everybody to see.

"We're building a simple course today and remaking it in a more difficult pattern tomorrow," she went on, cheerful and energetic.

"Have a good time," Ivy muttered, looking out over Samson's stall wall with a brush in her hand.

"Aren't you going to help?" Kate said in surprise. "Come on!"

"I actually have to wait for the vet," Ivy said.

"Don't be silly," Mia said, totally surprising herself. "He won't be here for another hour."

"I'm going to take Samson out for a walk while I'm waiting…" Ivy started before falling silent.

Suddenly, she realized that she was making a fool of herself in front of the others, and with an angry frown she left the stall. She slammed the door shut with a bang, which made Samson jump. Kate looked at her, eyebrows knitted.

"What's the matter with you?" she said to Ivy. "Did you get out on the wrong side of the bed today *too?*"

"I don't understand why I have to drag around a lot of heavy poles and obstacles that I can't jump over anyway," Ivy muttered grimly, throwing her brush into the bucket, "but sure, I'll help."

They all went together over to the riding track. Ivy's bad mood had infected the others, and nobody said anything as they started loading poles and obstacles onto the little cart and pulling it out into the ring.

"I can't believe you dared saying that," Linda said to Mia a little later, when they were standing at the far end of the ring. The plan indicated that they were to build an oxer there.

"I was so angry," Mia said, feeling a little proud of herself. She could hardly believe that she'd told cool and confident Ivy off!

"I wish I weren't so shy all the time," Linda puffed, lifting a red and white pole. "I almost never dare say anything. Even when I think something is wrong, I just keep my mouth shut, and then regret it later."

"I'm just like that," Mia said, "but I think you have to decide to dare."

"What do you mean?" Linda asked, watching Mia.

Mia fell silent, thinking for a while.

"Before I got here, I was totally sure that I would be stupider and more cowardly than anybody else. I was sure that everybody else would know a lot more than I do and have better horses, and –"

"I know what you mean," Linda eagerly interrupted. "I felt exactly the same!"

"But when I actually got here I realized that it wasn't like that. Everybody is good at some things and worse at others, just like Burly and me. And although Ivy sounds angry, I think she's mostly sad."

"What?" Linda said in surprise, looking at Mia with her eyebrows raised.

"Kate told me last night that Ivy and Emma are best friends, but just look what Emma's doing. She doesn't even talk to Ivy. She just fusses over Ricky all the time."

"I didn't even think about that," Linda said slowly. "I just thought that they were having fun together, all three of them, like you, me and Kate."

Mia shook her head and nodded toward the other end of the ring, where Ivy was walking by herself, counting the steps between two obstacles. Ricky and Emma were nowhere to be seen. Maybe they had already gone to get their horses ready. Kate walked over with the plan for the course. She smiled cheerfully and wiped sweat from her forehead. It was hot already, and the sun was shining down on the gravel-covered riding ring.

"Are you two standing there chatting instead of working? Now let's see if you managed to put the oxer in the right place. Hmm…"

"Oh, queen of the building of courses, we are your devoted slaves," Linda joked.

"Tell us if we have succeeded or failed. If we have failed, it will be our pleasure to beg for punishment," Mia continued in the same vein. Kate pretended to knit her eyebrows angrily.

"Well, I must admit you've succeeded," she said after glancing at her paper and the obstacle. "Good for you. You'll escape beheading today too. But if Prince just tears down one pole it's the axe for you!"

"But it can't be our fault if His Royal Highness is careless with his legs," Mia protested. Kate gave her a haughty look.

"His Royal Highness Prince Sourpuss *only* misses

obstacles that were faulty to begin with. And therefore, ladies, it's you who will be in trouble if he happens to touch a pole. But for now, this looks quite okay."

"Oh, thank you," Linda squeaked.

"You're all too kind," Mia whined, and all three broke into hysterical laughter. Ivy gave them a questioning look from the other side of the ring without even a hint of a smile. Then she turned on her heel and walked briskly toward the stable.

CHAPTER 9

Outside the stable, when Mia mounted Burly she felt a little nervous. But when she, Linda and Kate were walking toward the riding ring a moment later she felt better immediately.

When they came into the ring her mouth went dry from nervousness again. Greta was setting up a video camera!

"Oh, no," Kate moaned. "Are you kidding? I don't want to be filmed."

"What's the problem?" Emma said, tossing her head and smiling. "You can learn a lot by watching yourself jump."

"I don't want to be taped either," Mia said, patting Burly's neck. "I'm sure I'm going to fall off right in front of the camera."

"Shhh," Linda hissed, "don't say that. It'll turn into something my grandpa calls a self-fulfilling prophecy."

"Self-fulfilling what? What's that mean?" Emma asked, opening her big eyes even wider.

"Well, if you keep thinking that you're going to fall off, you will, sooner or later," Linda explained. "But if you think you're going to ride the course without a hitch, you can actually do that instead."

"I always think that the night before a competition," Emma said, patting Jolly, "but then we usually do fine, too."

"It's called psychological training," Greta explained when she heard what the girls were discussing. "Many athletes use that. I thought that we could talk about it in a theory class."

"And if I were you, I'd get that blade of hay out of Burly's tail," Kate suddenly said to Mia. "If you have straw in your tail you might fall off, or at least that's how the old wives' tale goes."

"Stop it right now," Mia moaned before jumping off and carefully combing Burly's thick tail with her fingers.

She thought that she had brushed Burly's tail very carefully before, but there actually was one blade that she'd missed. Mia took it off and hoped that both Linda and Kate were wrong, since Greta still seemed determined to film them while they were jumping.

Across the track, Ricky was walking Mistral around. The chestnut still walked with his head high, but seemed calmer now than he had before.

Ricky talked to him the whole time, and Mia thought that Ricky actually had started to be nicer to his horse since the beginning of the week. Maybe Ricky was shy too sometimes, and maybe that was why he always tried to impress everybody.

"Start riding. We're not here to enjoy the sunshine, everybody," Greta called to them before she started looking through the camera.

"Okay, Prince Sourpuss, let's make our mark on movie history," Kate muttered, winking at Mia, who felt butterflies flying around in her stomach.

She tried to forget the camera, but it wasn't easy and Burly used her uncertainty as much as he could. He felt stiff and bored and he didn't try at all. Mia worked until she was soaked in sweat, but he still didn't walk any better. Finally, she hit him behind the girth with her crop, but the only result was that he angrily bucked in protest.

"Come on over here, Mia," Greta called. Mia thought she was going to get a lecture about Burly having to move forward before he could jump, but Greta said something completely different.

"Dismount, loosen the girth, and take him to that grass over there. But don't let him eat."

"What?" Mia said, staring at Greta. "Are you kidding?"

"Not at all," Greta smiled. "Just do it. Meanwhile, Emma can start jumping the course."

Emma nodded energetically and rode a little circle while the others moved their horses to stay out of her way. Jolly obediently galloped, and with her hands holding loose reins and flopping in her saddle Emma went for the first obstacle.

Mia slowly walked to the grass patch along the riding ring with Burly. She didn't understand a thing, but Burly suddenly seemed very happy. He hardly made it out on the grass before he peed.

Mia laughed.

"You ruffian," she said, patting him. "That's why you didn't want to walk."

Burly snorted and shook his head before he quickly tried to tear the reins out of Mia's hands and get a mouthful of the thick green grass. She quickly stopped him, tightened the girth and remounted.

Now he felt very different. He seemed a lot more eager, and it was as if he was suddenly wide awake.

"That's a good trick for a horse that usually has energy but suddenly seems to lack it," Greta said kindly to Mia while she watched Jolly and Emma. "Sometimes it works, sometimes not. Warm him up a little more, because you're up after Emma."

When Emma had jumped the course once, Greta started filming her second round. Emma actually collected her reins a little this time, and Jolly obediently and with ears pricked went for the obstacles. They made it around the course without a hitch, and Emma gave a satisfied smile as she slowed and patted Jolly's neck.

"Now it's Mia's turn," Greta said, nodding encouragingly.

Mia pressed Burly on and galloped toward the first obstacle. Burly did his best and jumped the entire course without hesitation. Suddenly Mia felt joy bubbling up inside her. This was what jumping should be like! When she started her second lap she didn't even care that Greta was filming them.

Burly jumped broadly and elegantly and Mia was so happy that she could have jumped off him and given him a big hug after the last obstacle, which was a very big triple bar.

This is the hardest course we have ever jumped and he didn't even touch a single pole, Mia thought happily as she walked Burly over to the others.

"Nice," Kate said cheerfully. "He really jumps well."

"Thanks," Mia puffed, patting Burly's neck while Linda trotted into the ring with Graygirl.

The mare snorted energetically and jumped a lot higher than she needed over the small obstacles, and Linda had some trouble staying in the saddle. After Linda and Graygirl rode their first round, Greta called them over, and Linda slowed down.

"That's enough for Graygirl," Greta said. "Now pat her and dismount at once. Considering her inexperience, and the fact that she jumped the entire course without missing a single obstacle, you've both done a very good job indeed."

"Okay," Linda said, getting down from Graygirl, who started rubbing her head against Linda's back.

"Ricky and Mistral, you're next," Greta said, and Ricky immediately approached her.

"Can't you raise the obstacles a little?" he asked, nodding toward the course. "This isn't even Easy B."

"Today, we're only jumping an easy course," Greta said softly. "You'll get to jump high tomorrow."

"But Mistral isn't really good with obstacles this low. He just gets careless and misses them."

"Let's see," Greta said. "Remember that he has a new bit. He has to get used to that before you can jump him higher."

Ricky shrugged, shortened his reins, set off on a gallop and went for the first obstacle. Mistral threw himself at it and jumped long and high over it. Then he flew around the course like a golden flash. Ricky was totally focused on aiding him across the obstacles instead of running around them.

After the last obstacle, Ricky galloped in a circle before he pulled the horse up. Mistral stopped obediently without throwing his head up as he usually did. Ricky rode over to Greta.

"I hate saying this, but it actually seems like he's throwing his head less now," Ricky said, smiling in some embarrassment. "Maybe it works the way you said after all."

Greta nodded.

"I also think he seems to be enjoying himself more. Ride another lap and I'll film you."

Ricky nodded and Mistral flew around the course once more. After them Kate and Prince were on. Prince jumped calmly and efficiently, as if he'd never done anything else, and Kate seemed very focused and rode beautifully. They got lots of praise from Greta, who of course filmed them too.

"That's a textbook example of how to ride a course," she said. "Well done, Kate."

"Imagine, he didn't tear down one single pole," Kate said, smiling from ear to ear. "It seems Prince Sourpuss is having a good day."

Just then Ivy came walking up. Without saying a word she sat down on the little bench by the course. She tore off a long blade of grass and started twisting it between her fingers.

"Well, that's it then," Greta said, taking the video camera off the stand. "After lunch we'll watch the film, and tonight you'll get to jump this course again, so you can immediately use what the film shows you. Well, Ivy, what did the vet say?"

"Samson isn't lame anymore," Ivy muttered.

Mia thought it was strange that she didn't seem the least bit happy. She would have been beside herself with happiness if Burly had been lame and then suddenly became healthy again.

"I can ride him as usual this afternoon," Ivy went on, "but there's no point saddling him up now, right?"

Mia looked over at Kate, who had a thoughtful furrow between her eyebrows. For a moment, it seemed that she was going to say something snide to Ivy, but then she turned Prince around toward the stable and walked away without a word. Mia followed her example on Burly.

Behind her, she could hear Emma's cheerful voice, "That's just great! I've been so worried. I could hardly jump before, because I was thinking so much about you and Samson."

"I'm still worried about him," Ivy said, "but it's going to be okay."

"I'm sure it will," Greta said warmly. "Take your sweaty horses in and hose them down. Then it's time for lunch. I think we're having Spaghetti Bolognese today."

CHAPTER 10

A few hours later, they all gathered in front of the TV; everybody except Emma, Mia noticed. Emma was lying in bed with a headache, Greta said, and Mia glanced at Ivy who was sitting next to Ricky on the sofa, looking smug.

Greta put the film in and turned the TV on, and everybody sat quietly and watched.

Mia could feel herself blushing down to her toes when she and Burly were jumping. They looked just terrible. She jumped every obstacle with mouth open and eyes staring and Burly looked like a fat yellow steamroller. It was awful!

But nobody else agreed.

"You looked great," Kate said in despair. "Just look at Prince and me. A little fat redhead on a spindly chestnut who hardly even manages to lift his legs."

"What about me," Linda moaned. "I'll never jump again in my life if that's how terrible we look. Graygirl can be a dressage pony instead."

"Oh, stop complaining," Ivy said haughtily. "You look that way every time you jump, you just don't know it. By the way, it doesn't matter how your face looks or if you're too fat. The important thing is how you ride," she went on.

"Well, that's unusually sound advice, coming from you," Kate mused, "but I guess it's just because you're not in the film yourself."

Everybody laughed and it was Ivy's turn to blush, but as soon as the laughter died down Ricky casually said, "I agree with Ivy. There's nothing to worry about. My dad often films me when I'm practicing and it's a big help."

Then it was Greta's turn to speak and Mia listened carefully. Greta criticized her for not driving enough, and going along for the ride around the course while Burly jumped on his own. But she also got praise for her fine position and soft hands.

Mia eagerly lapped up the praise and decided to pay more attention to driving Burly, but she knew it would be hard. After all, Burly was lazy by nature, and sometimes she felt she couldn't really deal with him.

Emma appeared at dinner. She looked tired but didn't seem to have a headache anymore. She was soon chatting in her usual manner.

After dinner they were supposed to go riding, but Greta suggested that they go for a swim instead, and almost everybody thought that was a better idea. It was very hot and nobody felt like riding, but Kate didn't want to swim. She wanted to stay at home instead with a good horse book that she'd found on Greta's shelves.

The book may have been just an excuse, however, because by the time Mia had gotten her swimsuit on, grabbed a towel from the drawer and was ready to leave, Kate was already fast asleep. Without Kate noticing anything Mia carefully took the book from the bed and put it on the little nightstand. Then she hurried down the stairs to the others, who were waiting in the hall.

A while later they all walked through the woods on their way down to the little lake close to the farm. They followed a winding path that went through the woods and then passed an old enclosed pasture.

The fence was rusty barbed wire and hung precariously between old, worn poles. Several poles had fallen, and Mia thought it was very sad.

Sometime long ago, somebody had sunk those poles down into the earth, sweating and working hard, to make it possible for cows to graze here during the summer months. Now the pasture was deserted and the forest was slowly recapturing the land.

Mia enjoyed the water, which was lukewarm and very still and calm. She swam out a bit and then lay floating on her back, staring up into the blue sky and thinking about nothing at all.

After a while she squinted toward the shore. Ricky was sitting and talking to Emma. He looked pale and spindly next to Emma, who wore a bright yellow bikini. It shone against her tan and her hair looked white as snow from this distance.

Ivy was several yards off from them, talking to Greta, and Linda had followed Mia's example and swum quite far from the shore.

While she was floating out there Mia thought about Emma and Ricky. She wondered if Ricky really was as interested in Emma as Emma was in him. He almost seemed embarrassed at her eager tries to get his attention.

Mia thought to herself that she actually wasn't jealous of Emma anymore. It was the other way around now. This stuff with boys just seemed to be a hassle. It was probably just as well to keep away from them for as long as possible...

"Horses are better," she said loudly, and Linda, who had just swum up to her, looked at her in surprise.

"What?" she asked, stopping to tread water next to Mia.

"I said, horses are better. They're about one thousand times better and nicer than boys."

Linda nodded.

"Yes, I think I have to agree with you on that point. Or maybe it's just because we're so shy and awkward all the time that we think so. Those cool girls never seem to have any problems."

"Don't you think?" Mia said thoughtfully. "I actually think they do."

"Yes, that's true," Linda said after a while. "I wasn't thinking."

Mia and Linda smiled at each other in secret understanding, and Mia thought it was nice to have a friend like Linda, somebody who actually understood how it felt to be shy instead of just cheerfully outgoing all the time.

Suddenly there was a low rumble and Mia saw a dark wall of threatening clouds on the horizon. She quickly swam for the shore and Linda followed.

"Are you afraid of thunder?" Linda asked as they swam, and Mia nodded.

"A little. Anyway, I don't like the idea of being in the middle of the lake when the lightning starts."

While Linda and Mia swam for the shore the others stood up, got their things together and started walking homewards. Greta stayed on the shore, waiting for them, and both girls hurried out of the water.

"Are we going to take the horses in when we get back?" Linda asked with worry in her voice.

"Yes, if Nick hasn't already…"

The rest of Greta's answer was drowned out by another

heavy thunderclap, and Mia turned and looked out over the lake. Far off, the sky was a very dark blue, and suddenly the enormous cloud was split apart by a great flash.

"Oh, it looks closer than I thought," Greta exclaimed. "Come on, let's run!"

The others waited at the edge of the woods and they ran together up to the farm. Mia felt her stomach starting to ache from nervousness. It's one thing when there's thunder and you're inside a nice, safe house, but it's quite another when you're out in the middle of the storm, she thought in terror.

At that moment, the big yellow house appeared in front of them, and they had just the garden to run through. Heart pounding and completely soaked with sweat, Mia took the porch stairs in one great leap.

"What about the horses?" Linda said again. "We have to get them in."

"It's already done," said Greta's mom, who peered out through the open front door. "Come on in and I'll fix you some sandwiches and drinks. We seem to be in for a really big thunderstorm, according to the weather report."

Everybody felt relieved when they went up to their rooms and changed. Mia's legs were like jelly and she sank down on her bed, exhausted. Kate had just taken a shower and was trying to unravel her frizzy hair with a brush.

"Was the lake water cold?" she asked, making a pained face as the brush caught another tangle.

"No, it was really warm," Mia said, getting into a dry T-shirt. "But there's a thunderstorm."

"Yes, thank you, I noticed that. Nick came and woke me up earlier because he needed help getting all your horses in. And it was right when I was dreaming that Prince and I were jumping in the World Championships. Now I'll never know how we did."

"It's probably just as well," Mia smirked, and then had to duck quickly when the hairbrush came flying through the air.

A while later, Mia leaned out through the window and watched the almost black sky. It was very quiet and she couldn't even hear the blackbird that usually sat trilling in the lilac bush beneath their window.

Mia shuddered and closed the window. She didn't want the rain to come in when the storm arrived. Oh, how she hated thunderstorms!

In the next moment, a flash that made both girls jump lit the entire room. Mia quickly backed away from the window. Next, a deafening thunderclap made the windowpanes rattle. The door opened and Linda peered in.

"Wow," Kate exclaimed. "I wonder what that flash hit."

"Maybe the silo," Linda squeaked with a voice that sounded as if it came from a mouse. "That's where it usually hits at Grandpa's."

Linda face was pale and her big blue eyes looked even bigger than usual.

"Come on, let's go grab a sandwich. I thought I heard something about them when I helped Nick with the horses," Kate said and they hurried down the stairs.

In the kitchen, the others were already sitting around the big table. Greta served up the food, which tasted great after their exertion.

Mia felt a lot better. In the well-lit, cozy kitchen, with everybody around her and Nick joking in his usual way, the thunder suddenly seemed less frightening. Yes, everybody went silent from time to time, when some great flash made the kitchen lamp blink or when a heavy rumble crossed the farm, but apart from that it was as if nothing existed outside the four walls of the kitchen.

Also, that shy silence that had been there before everybody got to know each other was completely gone. Now everybody talked at once, and sometimes neither Nick nor Greta could make themselves heard.

As usual, Mia mostly sat silent and listened, but she didn't feel like an outsider now, the way she always did in school or at the recreation center at home. No, here she was one of the gang, and when she thought about that it made her warm inside.

Even Ivy and Emma were nice, she thought, and maybe Ricky wasn't so bad either. He probably had a hard time with Mistral, and even if she didn't like his rough methods it was hard to not like him.

Kate asked Nick a few things about the trotters and he gladly answered.

"By the way, have any of you ever driven a horse?" Nick asked, and the room went silent.

"No, never," Emma admitted. "I don't think I'd

dare. It seems to be so fast when you're trotting," she added, snuggling close to Ricky, who blushed from her attention.

"And the rest of you?" Nick asked, looking around the table.

He looked questioningly at Mia and, feeling put on the spot, she didn't dare to do anything but nod.

"We have a sulky at home, so I've tried with Burly a few times. And Dad drives him in the woods in the winter."

"Oh, can we go for a ride with a horse and cart some day?" Emma asked, opening her big blue eyes wide and staring at Mia. "That would be great! I'm sure I'd dare to sit in a cart with Burly. He seems so nice."

"Well, I don't have a cart or harness here," Mia said quietly, "or it would have been fun."

"So can't we use a sulky?" Emma suggested, and Kate moaned.

"Burly isn't a trotter, silly! Fjord horses are workhorses."

"And in a sulky there's only room for one person," Ivy said, sounding irritated with her friend.

"Oh," Emma said, blushing. "I didn't know."

Then the conversation moved back to jumping again and Mia let out her breath. It was true that she could have driven a little with Burly, but driving was something she did at home, and mostly to give Burly something else to do. She was here to learn to jump.

After hearing Emma and Ivy's comments about Burly,

she realized they probably still didn't take her seriously. She was sure they didn't mean to be haughty or nasty, but for them, a Fjord horse wasn't a jumper! She'd just have to show them they were wrong.

Mia stared out through the window at the rain falling from the dark sky, and promised herself to give it all she had. One day, she would learn to jump very well.

CHAPTER 11

"Isn't it strange that today is the next to last day?" Linda said at breakfast the next morning. "Imagine, we've been here for four days already."

"Don't say that," Kate moaned. "I don't want to go home!"

"Don't you?" Mia asked in surprise.

"No, because for the rest of the summer I'll be babysitting the terrible twins, and that's the worst punishment possible," Kate said sadly, spreading butter on a piece of bread.

"Oh, little kids are wonderful," Emma protested. "I'd love to work at a kindergarten when I've finished school. I love little kids with their round cheeks and… They're just gorgeous."

She swept her bangs away from her forehead and smiled at Kate, who made an ugly face in return.

"You can come home with us and take care of the twins," she said, licking the butter from her fingertips. "Once you've been with them for an hour, I promise you won't want to see a kid again for the rest of your life."

"I wish I had brothers and sisters," Linda said. "It's so boring being alone all the time. Imagine having someone to do things with. That would be great!"

"Well, okay," Kate muttered. "I'd almost rather die than admit this, but sometimes the kids are nice, and we actually do have some fun at home, too. Now and then, anyway."

At that moment, Ricky entered the kitchen. A cute girl followed him, about fifteen years old, with long dark hair and big brown eyes. She was dressed in a simple white T-shirt and a pair of leather-lined, light green jodhpurs.

The conversation ended and the kitchen fell silent. Everybody stared at the newcomer in surprise and Mia suddenly felt drab in her old beige riding pants and her worn favorite shirt.

"This is Angelica," Ricky said, waving nonchalantly toward the girl. "She's here to check out Mistral."

"Are you selling him?" Ivy said in surprise, and Ricky nodded.

"Yes, if Angelica wants to buy him. I'm getting tired of riding ponies anyway. I want a big horse and my coach has found one that we're going to have a look at next week."

"Haven't you finished breakfast yet?" Greta exclaimed. She had come into the kitchen right after Ricky and Angelica. "You'll have to hurry if you want to ride before lunch."

Mia had butterflies in her stomach when she thought about the fact that they were going to jump, but now it wasn't nervousness she felt, but joy.

The night before they had ridden dressage in the indoor ring, since the rain never let up. Burly had done excellently and Mia looked forward to jumping the course they had done yesterday one more time.

Last night, lying in her bed, she had thought everything through very carefully. She had decided exactly how she wanted to ride and tried to imagine what Burly would do if she did this or that. Greta had said that you could encourage yourself beforehand, and Mia was very curious to see if this worked.

The video had helped her too, she thought as she placed her empty cup in the dishwasher, because one thing was for sure: today she planned to keep her mouth shut as she jumped!

Outside, the sun was shining once more and the sky was clear and blue. Mia squinted in the bright light and thought of her dad, who was probably working on the hay at home. Nick had grumbled about the rain last night, since it had fallen right on his newly mowed hay. But with a little luck everything would be okay, as long as it dried up today and there were no more showers.

Mia wondered if it had rained at home too. She hadn't called her parents in a couple of days, she realized with surprise. She, who always used to be homesick all the time, had hardly thought about her folks since… she actually couldn't remember. When had she spoken to her mom?

Mia agreed with Kate – she didn't want to go home either! Of course, it would be nice to sleep in her own bed and get away from Kate's snoring, Mia thought, giggling to herself. But at the same time, she was having more fun now than she'd ever had before.

When she walked toward the stable with the others, she suddenly felt how much she liked them and how empty her days would be without them. Like Linda, Mia was an only child, and even if Tessa came home from Italy soon it could get lonely sometimes.

Mia sighed deeply and went into the stable. She heard Burly neigh and quickly switched her train of thought. She brushed him and was just going to put his saddle on when Angelica stopped outside the stall. She looked at Burly for a long time without saying anything. Mia didn't speak either.

She already knew what she thought of Angelica. She's undoubtedly one of those stuck-up people who don't like Fjord horses, and think they're useless, Mia thought sourly and tightened the girth rashly enough for Burly to cough in surprise.

"I like your horse," Angelica said at that moment, and Mia gave her a surprised look.

"What?" she said, not sure if she'd heard correctly. "What did you say?"

"I like Fjord horses," Angelica said cheerfully. "The first horse I had was a Fjord horse that I borrowed from my cousin. He was just wonderful! He wasn't very good at jumping, but still, he was the cutest in the world. He was unbelievably strong, though. I didn't have a chance when he dragged me across the yard."

"Burly's the same," Mia admitted, and suddenly the ice was broken. "He's a real Greedy Gus, and I think he'd eat himself to death if I weren't around to stop him."

"But he's so lean and beautiful," Angelica remarked. "Do you ride him a lot?"

"Twice a day during the summer," Mia said, bridling Burly who obediently gaped, making it easy to put the bit in his mouth.

"And Greta says he's a good jumper," Angelica said. "It's going to be fun to see him. But I guess I'll have my hands full with Mistral."

"Are you going to ride in the class?" Mia asked. Angelica nodded.

"Yes, Dad wants to see if I can handle Mistral. I tried riding him before Ricky bought him, but we couldn't buy him then since we hadn't sold my first pony. But now she's finally sold to a great family, so I hope we can buy Mistral. He's just gorgeous. He's been my dream for years!"

107

When Mia heard Angelica talking about Mistral she felt warm inside. She knew that he'd have a good life at Angelica's, and she hoped for both Angelica's and Mistral's sake that everything worked out.

"So what happened to the Fjord horse?" Kate said, suddenly sticking her head up from behind Prince's door. "Was he sold too?"

"No, my cousin still owns him," Angelica said. "He often says that a stable isn't complete without a Fjord horse."

Mia smiled to herself. That sounded good. She'd make sure to remember to tell Tessa that when she came home.

Out in the riding ring, Greta had raised the obstacles, and when Mia saw them she felt her stomach turn. She had never jumped this high with Burly before. Of course she thought that he could manage the obstacles, but was *she* up to it? She, who had hardly jumped a course before she came to Edinburgh four days ago...

"What silly little obstacles," she heard Ivy say behind her. "I thought Greta said we'd jump high today."

"Me too," Emma agreed. "I don't think that's barely an Easy A course."

"Well, it's high enough for Graygirl and me, anyway," Linda said. "I think I'll ask Greta to lower the obstacles for us."

"Yes, well, but then you're only beginners," Ivy said, sounding nonchalant and haughty in the way Mia hated.

"I guess it's just as well that Mia and you jump a little

lower than the rest of us, since you're not as advanced yet. It would be terrible if you got hurt."

Ivy probably didn't mean to sound as haughty as she actually did, but Mia felt hot anger rising inside. She was going to show Ivy and Emma what she and Burly could do!

Everybody got to warm up their horses any way they liked, while Greta watched and gave advice. Mia rode intently and tried to drive Burly all the time. She made tempo changes and halts and Burly was obedient and attentive.

Kate and Prince jumped first. Prince was in a terrible mood and knocked down poles everywhere. Greta had to rebuild almost the entire course when Kate was finished, and Emma and Ivy, waiting for their turn next to Mia, snorted loudly.

"If he could just lift his legs, he'd be a great pony," Ivy said to Emma, who nodded in agreement. Mia noted that they seemed to be best friends again.

"Kate ought to concentrate more when she rides," Emma said, knitting her forehead. "He isn't collected at all."

Mia looked sideways at Linda, who was beet red from holding in her laughter.

Keeping the horses collected was something that Greta had talked a lot about the night before, when they rode dressage. It meant that the horse should be well-reined, work with its back, and get its hind legs in under itself. It wasn't easy to ride your horse that way and it seemed that Emma liked the expression, Mia thought as she turned away. She didn't want Emma to see her smiling.

Kate and Prince finished their second round without knocking down a single pole, and Emma nodded wisely.

"She rode better this time," she said to Ivy. "I think it's very important that she keep Prince collected."

"Your turn, Emma. Then it's Ivy," Greta called out. Ivy trotted off on Samson to warm him up some more while Emma straightened her helmet. Then, with flopping reins and legs, she rode out to the obstacles.

Jolly looked at the obstacles with interest while slowly trotting around, and then Emma managed to put her into a slow canter.

Emma immediately went for the first obstacle and Jolly almost jumped from a standing position. Then she ran around both the second and the third obstacles before Emma finally managed to stop her at the far end of the course.

"You have to shorten your reins," Greta called. "Shorten the reins and press on, Emma. Collect her and don't let her become too long."

"I think Emma ought to concentrate more," Kate said firmly to Linda and Mia. "She really ought to keep Jolly more collected," she said, suddenly looking at Mia and Linda with surprise. They couldn't keep a straight face anymore. Both of them were laughing like crazy.

"What's the matter with you two?" Kate asked, but no one could answer, and after shaking her head she started walking Prince slowly. He was soaked with sweat from jumping in the heat.

"She probably thinks we're out of our minds," Linda managed to say, and Mia nodded in agreement.

"We'd better ride over to her and explain," Mia said, shortening her reins. "Come on!"

Emma was done and now it was Ivy and Samson's turn. They galloped around the course and Mia had to admit that Ivy rode well. Samson had no chance of breaking out and he jumped all the obstacles without knocking off a single pole.

"I suppose that was the fastest round today," Ricky said. He was standing by the fence, chewing on a blade of grass, while Angelica trotted around on Mistral a few yards away.

"Yes, Ivy is very good," Emma said a little haughtily, and Mia had to ride away from them to keep from laughing again.

She couldn't understand why she was in such a giggly mood.

After Ivy, it was Angelica's turn to jump with Mistral, and Mia pulled Burly up to watch her. Angelica rode Mistral in a very different way from Ricky. She kept her hands low and still and didn't saw on Mistral's mouth all the time. Instead, she talked soothingly to him, and when he tried to rush off she rode in a circle, trotting for a while until he had calmed down.

A gray-haired man in his forties was standing by the fence. He didn't say very much, but he was watching Angelica and Mistral. Mia thought that he must be

Angelica's dad, and when Angelica finished jumping he went out and spoke with Greta.

After that, he, Ricky and Angelica went back to the stable with Mistral. Angelica met Mia's eye and quickly winked. Mia smiled to herself. She knew that everything had worked out.

"Do you need some help lowering the obstacles?" Emma offered, and Greta gave her a surprised look.

"Lower the obstacles?" she said. "Why? A few people haven't jumped yet."

"But only Burly and Graygirl are left," Ivy said, smiling at Mia. "They can't jump as high as the rest of us, can they? Fjord horses aren't really jumpers, and Graygirl is very young."

"I'd really like you to lower the obstacles for me," Linda said, and Greta nodded.

"Yes, I was actually thinking about that, but you can manage this course," she went on, looking at Mia.

"And I want to jump it," Mia said, shortening her reins.

"So do it," Greta said encouragingly. "Go for it!"

Mia could feel butterflies in her stomach, but she still managed to smile at Emma and Ivy before she rode off.

"Is she really…" she heard Ivy's voice behind her and Mia thought that she should really thank Ivy, because Ivy always managed to tease Mia enough to fill her with rage. If she hadn't been so angry, maybe she wouldn't have dared jumping so high.

In a slow canter, she rode Burly toward the first

obstacle. Afterwards she couldn't really remember much more than the fantastic feeling of flying over the obstacles. Burly really went all out and jumped high and sure, like a good competition pony.

Mia felt everything just fall into place. She rode as if in a dream, and when she'd finished her second round it felt like she could have gone on jumping forever.

"Nice!" Greta called out, and Mia suddenly heard applause.

It was Kate and Linda who were clapping, perched on their horses. Mia blushed until her cheeks burned when Kate yelled, "Great!"

Mia proudly looked around as she rode back to her friends, but Ivy and Emma had already ridden back to the stable. Typical, when she had done so well and showed that she and Burly were as good as they were. But it really didn't matter, Mia thought, patting Burly's neck. She had proven to herself that she and Burly could jump, and that was the important thing.

Graygirl got to jump low and easy, and she collected lots of praise when she made it around the course. Afterwards, the three friends walked their horses back to the stable.

"Hey, we're so good," Kate hollered, patting Prince's neck.

"Well now, Prince knocked down every obstacle in his first round," Mia teased, but Kate just smiled back at her.

"Who cares! He only jumps when somebody's filming him. That's the real problem. I'll ask dad to bring the video camera tomorrow, and I'm sure Prince will fly over every obstacle."

✧ ✧ ✧ ✧

After lunch the riders had a couple of hours off, and Kate immediately lay on her bed and fell asleep with her horse book over her nose. Mia snuck out of the room and went to Linda's. She was in one of the two small rooms at the far end of the top floor.

The room was small and cramped. A bed and a little chest of drawers almost filled the space, and the only window was small, placed high on the wall and formed like a half-circle.

Mia guessed that this room had once been a closet or a storage room.

"Do you want to sunbathe for a while?" Mia suggested. She had just taken out her bathing suit and a big towel.

Linda nodded, and a while later they were out in the yard. They found a good place for their towels next to a lilac hedge, and Linda squinted at the sun.

"Wow, it's hot here. We ought to go down to the lake."

"I can't," Mia said, lying down on her towel. "I'm completely exhausted after this morning."

"I wonder how we're going to do in the jumping competition tomorrow," Linda said. "I just hope Graygirl and I don't make fools of ourselves. Mom said that Grandpa might be coming."

"I'm sure you'll do fine," Mia said encouragingly. "Remember that Graygirl's young. When you're a beginner, you don't have to be perfect. I bet your grandpa knows that."

"Hey, did you notice how Emma smiled at the camera

114

the whole time Greta was recording us?" Linda giggled. "Like a supermodel! I thought I'd…" she was going to continue when they heard quick steps and raised voices from the gravel path on the other side of the hedge.

"But you said…" they heard Emma's agitated voice.

"I never said we were dating," Ricky said more calmly. "You're just imagining it."

"Yes you did, and you said it was over with Angelica."

"Angelica isn't my girlfriend," Ricky hissed. "Don't yell like that, everybody can hear you."

"I don't care," Emma snorted and Mia could hear that she was close to tears. "You just kept leading me on."

"I never promised anything," Ricky said. "Calm down! Angelica just came here to check Mistral out, but I don't want us to…"

The voices died away and Linda and Mia looked at each other. Mia could feel the corners of her mouth twitching. It was like some silly TV soap opera, she thought, and Linda seemed to agree.

"What do you know," Mia said. "At this camp, there's excitement and romance!"

"And I thought Ricky was really cute when I first came here," Linda said, "but now I don't like him at all. He's so annoying when he's trying to impress everybody all the time."

"Yeah," Mia said, nodding.

"At first, I just thought his self-confidence was an act," Linda went on, "but now I'm starting to think he might be that haughty and self-assured for real."

Before Mia could answer they heard running steps on the gravel path and Mia and Linda immediately fell silent and pretended to be asleep. They heard somebody sobbing, and when Mia turned her head she saw Emma disappearing up toward the house.

Mia couldn't help feeling sorry for her. It seemed Ricky was a bad egg, just as Kate had said from the start.

"Even so, I wish I could get to experience something exciting and romantic sometime," Linda added, sighing.

"I don't know," Mia said thoughtfully. "If love's *that* much of a hassle, maybe I'll stick to Burly."

CHAPTER 12

Later that afternoon, Greta told the group that first they
would do a combined outdoor riding and scavenger hunt,
and then grill hot dogs down at the beach.

"Scavenger hunt? But that's for little kids," Ivy
grumbled, rolling her eyes at Emma when Greta didn't
see. But she didn't say anything more, and about an hour
later they were all in the saddle.

"I've made two-person teams," Greta said. "Kate will
ride with Linda, Ivy with Emma and Ricky with Mia. The

117

scavenger hunt is in the woods here behind the farm, and you just have to follow the white plastic ribbons to find the questions."

"Do we have to do this if we don't want to?" Ivy muttered, looking over at Greta. "I'd rather practice dressage or jumping."

"Of course you can, but I think it's important to do a variety of things with your horse, rather than just demanding the same things of him or her all the time. Horses need to get out and have a good time every now and then, just like people. You jumped this morning, we rode a tough dressage yesterday and we'll have a competition to end the course tomorrow afternoon. Don't you think that's enough?"

Ivy didn't answer. Instead, she looked down at Samson's neck and fussed a little with the reins. It was awkwardly quiet for a while.

"Oh, come on," Kate said, clicking her tongue at Prince. "Where do we start?"

"Behind the indoor ring," Greta said. "Mia and Ricky will go first. Come on, I'll show you."

The mood suddenly lightened, and although Ivy was still sulking, nobody but Emma cared anymore.

Each team started at five-minute intervals, and Mia and Ricky rode their horses in a walk toward the woods as the first team. Ricky didn't say very much, and at first Mia wished that she had been teamed with Kate or Linda instead, but Greta had explained that she wanted to pair Burly with Mistral, to show Mistral a really calm and safe horse.

Mia wasn't sure that she'd understood correctly, but she thought that Ricky hadn't looked happy at all. Of course, he hadn't protested, but Mia still wasn't too cheerful. He rode with her just because he had to, not because he thought it was fun, she thought, clenching her teeth. If he was going to sulk, well, she could do that too.

As soon as they'd left the others behind, however, things were a little better. She and Ricky chatted about this and that, and it was easy to follow the white plastic ribbons, which were placed just a few yards apart. Greta had given Mia a paper and a pencil and the first two questions were simple.

"That obstacle is a palmetto," Ricky said, pointing his crop at the drawing. And of course Mia could answer the next question.

"Fjord horses are from Norway," she said cheerfully, writing a number two in the correct space.

"Did you know that Fjord horses are called Norwegian Thoroughbreds?" Ricky asked. Mia looked at him.

"No, I never heard that," she said, shaking her head. "How do you know?"

"Our blacksmith told me," Ricky said. "Look. The path gets better up there. Let's trot and get rid of all these darned insects."

As soon as they could, they let their horses trot. The path was soft, and they enjoyed the pleasant smell of pine needles mixed with sun-warmed horses. Mia stroked Burly's neck and he snorted and shook his head. She felt very happy and was enjoying herself. She and Ricky actually had a good time together. She never would have believed that, she thought, sneaking a look at the cream-colored horse beside her.

Mistral snorted and it seemed as if he wanted to break into a gallop, but Ricky talked soothingly to him and kept him at a trot. Mia thought that even if Ricky could be quite tough sometimes he seemed to have changed a lot during their days here. Or maybe it was because he was going to sell Mistral to Angelica, she considered. Maybe he didn't really care that much anymore, if his horse was being sold anyway.

The next question was about how long the crop should be at a jumping competition, and once Mia and Ricky decided on 30 inches they moved on to the left up another narrow path. Mia had a distinct feeling that they were riding in a circle, and she guessed that they would come out on the other side of the farm when they'd finished the hunt.

Suddenly they heard a motor roaring.

"What's that?" Mia said in surprise. She automatically shortened Burly's reins. "A chainsaw?"

"I thought it sounded like a motorcycle," Ricky said. "I saw tracks from one a little further down. Let's hope we don't meet it, because –"

At that moment, two young guys came roaring at top speed around the turn just about ten yards in front of them. They quickly stopped with engines screaming and brakes squealing when they saw the horses, but it was too late. Mistral had already reared onto his hind legs and, in the next moment, he turned on the spot and bolted away along the path. Ricky couldn't stop him.

"Are you out of your minds?" Mia shouted at the two boys before turning Burly around and hurrying after Mistral.

Burly galloped quickly, but of course couldn't catch up with Mistral, who had gotten a head start. Soon Mia had to pull Burly up, since she couldn't see where Mistral had gone.

There where lots of small winding paths, and she couldn't be sure that Mistral had followed the same route back.

She heard a horse neigh, and Linda and Kate appeared behind a couple of big spruce firs.

"There you are!" Kate called. "Hurry! Mistral has gone through!"

Mia galloped over to her friends, who had already turned and were trotting back again.

"What do you mean, 'gone through'?" she panted when she and Burly caught up with Kate. "Where is he?"

"Mistral came galloping up to us, and when he saw us he was so scared that he turned and ran straight into the woods where there's a marsh," Kate panted.

"Why was he bolting like that?" Linda asked, pulling Graygirl up.

"Was he scared?" Kate said. Mia nodded.

"Yes, there were two motorcycles," she said, and in that second she saw Mistral a little further in among the trees.

He had gone down to his chest in the mud and was fighting desperately to break free. Ricky, muddy from his head to his toes, was standing on firm ground in front of Mistral with the reins stretched as far as they would go. It seemed he was trying to help his horse by pulling him up by the bridle, but of course that was impossible. Mistral was stuck too tightly.

"I'll ride for help," Kate shouted, galloping homewards while Mia and Linda stopped, dismounted and tied their horses to two trees.

Mia carefully went closer while Linda stayed with Graygirl and Burly. The ground was soggy and her shoes flopped, and for every step she took, her feet sank a couple of inches. In one spot her feet went so deep that she got wet and muddy all the way up to her knees.

Ricky kept tearing at the reins and Mistral threw his head in desperation as he tried to kick free from the terrible stuff he was caught in.

"Stupid horse, stop kicking. You'll just sink even further, you fool!" Ricky roared. Mia could hear that his voice was tense and hard from fear.

"Calm down," she said, putting her hand on Ricky's arm. "Stop pulling. It doesn't help."

Ricky stiffly stared at her, an angry wrinkle between his eyebrows, but Mia could see his lower lip trembling and she could tell he was scared.

"Go sit over there with Linda," she said, trying to sound determined and calm at the same time. "Kate's gone for help. We can't do anything for him right now anyway."

"We've got to get him up," Ricky protested hoarsely. "Or he'll drown in the mud."

"I don't think he will, but the more he kicks, the more tired he'll get. It's better if he saves his strength until we can lift him out. Now go over to Linda and sit on that rock next to Burly," Mia said calmly, and Ricky let out a deep sigh.

Then he reluctantly gave her the reins and limped over to Linda.

"Are you hurt?" Linda asked, and Mia heard Ricky mutter that Mistral had kicked him when he jumped off.

"There, there, boy," Mia said to Mistral, trying to sound as reassuring and calm as she could. "Everything's going to be fine, there, there…"

It felt like an eternity before Mistral stopped throwing himself back and forth, but finally he started listening to the quiet, friendly voice that was talking so softly to him.

He threw his head one last time and then became very still while he drew short, wild breaths. His nostrils were wide open, his eyes full of fear, and his entire body soaked with mud and sweat.

He looked wide-eyed at Mia, who kept trying to soothe him with nonsense words and rhymes, and it seemed as if he was listening to her voice. Mia hoped he would keep still. The more he could save his strength, the better.

Soon, Greta came galloping on Jolly, along with Kate on Prince and Ivy on Samson. When Mistral saw the other horses he started throwing his head again. His eyes rolled and he neighed in a heart-rending way. Then he started kicking again to break free, but the only thing that happened was that he sank even lower in the mud that now reached almost up to the saddle.

"How are we going to get him out?" Ricky asked Greta. "We have to do it now!"

"I'll call the fire department," Greta said, quickly getting her cell phone out.

She dialed a number and then it was quiet. A few seconds later, she shook her phone, trying again and again.

"It's not working!" she moaned at last. "The battery's dead. I'll have to ride home and phone from there. The farm is just a few hundred yards away."

"The question is, can the fire department get into these woods," Kate said silently, and everybody looked around.

The woods around the little marsh were mostly pine trees, growing close together, and there were big rocks everywhere. Mia remembered that Greta had said something about this part of the woods having been a nature preserve for many years.

"They just have to!" Greta said. "They'll have to chop down the trees to get to Mistral if necessary. I'm riding home now."

"Wait a minute," Mia said, swallowing.

Her throat was dry from nervousness. But she knew that the plan she was going to suggest was the only thing they could do.

"Burly can pull Mistral out. We just have to make a harness for him."

"That's impossible!" Ricky said in disbelief. "Let's call the fire department."

"You shouldn't try to fix problems like this by yourself," Ivy said harshly and looked at Mia. "This isn't a movie and you're no heroine. Wait for the fire department instead."

Mia stared angrily at Ivy. Then she turned to Linda and Kate.

"I actually think it could work," Kate said slowly. "We can make a long rope from all our leathers, and fasten it to his saddle somehow. It should be possible."

"Stop it, girls. This is an impossible situation," Greta said emphatically. "I'm riding home now. Wait here and don't try anything stupid."

She turned Jolly and galloped away on the path, but when Mistral saw Jolly disappear he went into hysterics. He threw himself back and forth, neighed over and over again, and you could see lather on his neck.

"We have to get him out!" Kate exclaimed. "We can't wait for the fire department. He'll kill himself."

"Yes, let's do what Mia suggested," Linda said. "Here are Graygirl's leathers."

Ivy seemed undecided, but she finally dismounted and loosened her leathers. The girls managed to make a long leather rope and Mia asked them to lengthen the rope with everything they could find. At last, the rope was long enough.

"So how are you going to attach it to Mistral?" Ricky

said, still dubious. "You can't even get out to him without sinking down yourself."

"There's a little tree over there that's blown down. Bring it over here, and those big branches next to it," Mia said, pointing into the woods.

Ricky, Kate and Ivy helped while Linda took care of the horses, and soon the big branches and the old pine tree were lying as close to Mistral's left side as possible. Mistral stared at them with big black eyes, but he stayed very still, without protesting. Maybe he doesn't have the strength to fight anymore, Mia thought.

Ricky carefully lay down on his stomach, pulling himself over the dark and muddy water to his horse. Mistral threw his head but didn't kick, and Ricky actually succeeded in tying the long rope under Mistral's girth on his left side.

"So how are we going to pull the rope under him?" Ivy asked. "This is impossible, don't you see?"

"We have to pull him up and sideways," Mia said decisively. "We can't pull him straight up, and forward is just more mud. It might even get deeper. Dad had two heifers that went through this a couple of years ago. The fire department pulled them up sideways, but then, they had real harnesses and stuff."

"Exactly," Ivy said. "What will you do if it doesn't work? Suppose that…"

"Do you have a better idea?" Kate angrily hissed at Ivy. "If not, why don't you just shut up! Get out of here if you're just going to make problems all the time. I'm so tired of your whining that I'm just about ready to push you down in the marsh, too, just so you know!"

Ivy sulked quietly and went over to Samson while Ricky carefully pulled himself to firm ground. He gave both ends of the rope to Mia, who had backed Burly up as close to Mistral as she dared.

His hooves were squelching and Mia could see that he too was sinking down into the muddy ground. She broke out in a cold sweat when she thought about Burly getting stuck in the treacherous mud too, but she tried to stay calm.

As quickly as she could, she tied the two ends of the rope to the girth on both sides with trembling hands. Then she tightened the girth an extra hole and thought to herself that it was a good thing that Burly always used a breastplate. If that held, and she thought it would, it would stop the saddle from sliding backwards, in spite of Mistral's weight. In a way, it was like a makeshift harness.

"Okay, honey, let's go," Mia said at last, clicking her tongue at Burly.

Burly sighed deeply. Then he used all his power and started pulling. It was as if he understood that this was a matter of life and death. He was very calm, although Mistral was fighting and snorting in the marsh behind him and his own hooves kept sinking deep down in the wet ground with every step.

Mia hardly dared to look, but step by step her horse made it to firmer ground, and now the tufts of grass were carrying his weight easily. Very slowly, inch by inch, Burly pulled Mistral out of the marsh.

Mistral, obviously realizing that he would soon be free, seemed to have gotten his strength back. He snorted and threw himself forwards and to the side simultaneously. At last, the strength in his movements made the marsh let go of him with a sucking sound.

Suddenly Mistral was lying on firm ground beside the marsh, kicking and snorting. As soon as he could, he rolled up on all fours, almost mowing down Ricky who had rushed over to catch his reins.

Soon, Ricky and Mistral were standing on the pine needle-covered path again. Mia loosened the leather rope from Burly and Ricky took the saddle off Mistral.

Mia felt happiness bubbling within her. She looked at Burly and he looked back at her with pricked ears and calm, clear eyes, as if he wanted to say, "That's nothing, really. You knew I could do it, didn't you?"

"What a horse you have," Ivy said, sounding impressed. "I never thought he could manage that."

"Me neither," Kate exclaimed. "That was just great! And you're great too, Mia. I'm impressed that you even dared to try!"

"Yes, Mistral never would have survived without you and Burly," Ricky sobbed, patting Mistral on his dirty neck. "Thank you, Mia. That was fantastic!"

"And brave," Linda added. "I never would have dared."

Mia nodded and threw her arms around Burly's sweaty

neck. She was so embarrassed by all the praise that she really didn't know what to say or do. Actually, it was Burly who had done everything and not her, she thought, hugging him again.

"Now let's go home," Linda said. "Did you hear that? Sirens!"

Far away, they could hear the sirens of the fire department, and Mia sighed with relief. Now there would be other people who could take care of Mistral and help him: Greta, Nick, the vet…

They started walking home along the path and Mia went last with Burly. She patted his neck over and over again. She and Burly had made it. Mistral seemed to be unhurt and Mia had finally gotten the chance to show Ivy what she and Burly were worth. That was the best part of this whole adventure.

Mia happily stroked Burly's neck and he threw his head to get rid of some pesky flies. He didn't seem excited at all by what had just happened, but was his usual self.

When he thought Mia didn't see, he tried to chew on a green twig, and Mia didn't bother trying to stop him. He deserved every snack he could grab, she thought. She smiled again, tired and very happy.

CHAPTER 13

Mia lay in her bed, staring up at the ceiling. Calm snores came from Kate's bed and Mia wished she were sleeping as deeply. She was totally awake, however, even though it was after one o'clock in the morning.

She tried thinking about getting up early next morning, and preparing Burly for the final jumping competition, but this didn't help at all. Instead, she felt even more awake when she realized how nervous she was. She wondered what Greta's course would be like.

They weren't going to see the plan for the course until just before jumping, like in a real competition. Then they would walk the course, doing everything as if it were "for real." Emma had even suggested that they wear riding jackets and white jodhpurs too, and everybody had liked that idea. Mia had called home to mom, asking her to bring her white jodhpurs and a white shirt, and Ivy was letting her borrow a riding jacket.

Ivy. Mia thought about how Ivy had surprised her over and over again during the evening. It was Ivy who had suggested that Mia borrow her jacket, since they were probably the same size.

Ivy had been nice and friendly to Mia all evening, not at all as haughty and scornful as earlier. If Ivy had been this nice all week they would probably had been good friends by now, but Mia couldn't really forgive some of the bad things Ivy had said about Burly during their time here.

She also suspected that Ivy's change might not be for real. It could be due to Burly's feat of pulling Mistral out of the swamp, because Mia had a feeling that both Emma and Ivy were the kind of girls who liked to be friends with the person who was most popular at the moment.

Mistral had survived his adventure with just a few scratches. The vet, a brunette woman in her thirties, had examined Burly for a long time but found nothing, apart from a few wounds and scratches on his legs. Of course Mistral was tired and black and blue, and Ricky had decided not to jump in the final competition tomorrow.

When they went down to the beach for their cookout, Linda whispered to Mia that Ricky really must love Mistral a lot, but later that night Mia heard him tell Ivy that he had mostly been worried about the fact that Angelica was buying him. It seemed Mistral was only insured for five thousand dollars, and Angelica was going to pay twice that amount if she bought him. If he had been hurt, there would have been no deal.

Mia sighed to herself. She didn't like Ricky, and although she tried over and over again to forget certain things about him, she just couldn't. She couldn't understand how he could regard Mistral as a lot of money and not as a good friend who might have died in that marsh. And she couldn't understand how he could sell Mistral to Angelica without being sad about losing his friend. Not that Angelica was a bad buyer. No, she seemed very nice, and Mia was sure she'd give Mistral a good home.

Mia, however, would never be able to sell Burly, not to anybody and not for all the money in the world.

It had been a nice evening anyway, Mia thought. Greta and Kate had built a fireplace with some big rocks while the others collected dry twigs and branches. Then they had cooked the hot dogs and talked about horses for hours. The lake had been as still as a mirror, and there was no wind at all when the sun slowly sank behind the horizon.

"What a great night," Kate said when they went back to the house after a late night swim in the warm water.

"Absolutely," Linda chimed in. "And what great five

days we've had. I'm going to miss you two so much when I get home."

"I'm going to miss you, too," Mia said. "Why don't you bring your horses and come see me? We have lots of pastures and I'm sure mom and dad will think it's fun."

"What a great idea," Kate squealed, elbowing Mia. "I'll be there right away. Little kids are a no-no at your place, right?"

"Little kids?" Mia had looked at her with surprise.

"Yes, I am *not* going to bring the twins."

"You won't have to," Mia laughed. "I can promise you that."

Mia turned in bed for at least the seventeenth time. She could hear her stomach rumbling. She was hungry, but the crackers and candy she and Kate had bought in the village a couple of days ago had been finished long ago. She wondered if she should sneak down to the kitchen. If she just got something to eat she was sure it would be easier to fall asleep.

Mia rose silently and pulled on her pants and a sweater. Then she padded out through the door and over to the stairs. It was quiet and calm and everybody seemed to be asleep.

The stairs were pitch dark, as opposed to the hallway outside their rooms, and Mia had to put her hand on the rail to keep from stumbling. She could feel her heart pounding, and when one step creaked loudly she thought everybody would wake up.

But nobody seemed to have heard her, and she took a few quick steps through the hall and into the kitchen. The light was better down here, and as soon as she was in the kitchen she turned the ceiling lamp on. She blinked at the light and hoped she hadn't woken anybody up.

Nick and Greta slept on this floor, but Mia knew that their bedroom was far from the kitchen. And anyway, she wouldn't be here for long; she'd just get something to eat.

When she peered into the fridge, she suddenly knew what she wanted. A glass of warm milk! Of course! Mom used to say that was the best sleeping potion in the world. Mia took out a carton of milk and found a little pan. She used a glass to measure the milk, poured it in the pan and turned the knob on.

This stove was slow, she knew from hearing Greta's mom complaining about it several times, so while the milk heated she went over to the window and peered out.

Outside, the yard was totally still in the blue summer night light, and through the open window she could smell the soft scents of summer. A soft breeze made the curtain move and Mia drew a breath. She suddenly felt so happy and satisfied with everything she had done during these five days. And tomorrow would be very exciting.

Mia got lost in her own thoughts and didn't notice what happened behind her, until a hissing sound and the angry stench of burned milk made her react. She quickly turned, rushed to the stove and grabbed the pan, but it was too late. The milk had boiled over and was running all over the stove. The smell was terrible and angry smoke billowed up.

Mia put the pan into the sink while she said some very angry words to herself. She had really done it this time. In the next moment, a deafening signal shrilled from a little white box in the ceiling. The fire alarm!

"Oh no!" Mia moaned, staring horrified at the ceiling.

It had to be the smoke from the stove that had started the alarm, and she had no idea what to do.

"I have to silence it somehow," she thought in confusion, looking around the kitchen.

A chair! She had to get up on a chair and try to find the Stop button as quickly as she could.

Before she could do anything the kitchen door slammed open and Nick came running in, dressed in pajamas. Right behind him was Greta in a nightshirt.

"Where's the fire?" Nick shouted. "Is anybody hurt?"

It was almost impossible to hear his voice in the persistent noise from the alarm. Mia waved her hands.

"No, no," she shouted. "Take it easy, it was just me…"

"We have to turn that blasted thing off," Nick shouted. He grabbed a chair and got up on it, but he was so rushed that the chair fell over and, with a heavy thud and a terrible scream, Nick hit the floor.

Now thuds could be heard from the top floor too. It was Ivy, Emma, Linda and Ricky who came rushing from their rooms.

"Is there a fire?" Emma squealed. "Should we run out?"

"I can smell smoke," Ivy added.

"Or some other nasty stuff," Linda screamed, holding her nose.

"Take it easy. There's no fire," Greta shouted at the top of her lungs. She was trying to scream louder than the alarm, which kept squealing although Nick was now up on the chair, trying to silence it.

"There's no fire," Mia screamed. "It was just me, trying to heat some milk."

"Heat milk?" Ricky roared. "In the middle of the night? But why in the world?"

"I can't silence this moronic thing!" Nick shouted. "Greta, get me a screwdriver!"

Greta ran off to get a screwdriver, but suddenly Nick hit the fire alarm with his fist, in pure anger, and it actually fell silent. The kitchen was suddenly quiet. Very quiet. Mia could feel herself blushing from her ears to her toes.

"Finally," Nick panted, getting down from the chair. "Now I'd like to hear everything from the beginning. What are you doing in the kitchen in the middle of the night, and why did the alarm go on?"

"I was just heating some milk," Mia said quietly, "and I forgot the pan…"

"Wow," Greta said, entering the room with a screwdriver in her hand. "You scared the living daylights out of us."

Emma started giggling.

"I thought the stable was on fire," she said, pushing her bangs off her forehead. "Good thing it was only some burned milk."

"I was hungry and I couldn't sleep," Mia went on.

"Why didn't you just call out for pizza instead?" Ricky

suggested, smiling. "That way, the rest of us could have stayed asleep."

After that, nobody could keep from laughing and Mia felt better when she thought about what good buddies she had. Nobody seemed angry with her for waking them in the middle of the night, even though she didn't know if she should laugh or cry about the whole mess.

"Well now, everybody" Greta said after a while, looking at her watch. "You'd better get back to sleep. Do you want something to eat, Mia?"

"I'm not hungry anymore," Mia said. "I'll just go back to bed again."

"Where's Kate, by the way?" Linda asked.

Ivy smiled. "I'm sure she's asleep," she said. "Kate is the sleepiest human being in the world."

At that moment, steps could be heard on the stairs and a newly awakened Kate stuck her head through the door. She looked around at all the people in the well-lit kitchen, yawned from ear to ear and asked, "What happened? Is there a fire?"

She was met by wild giggling, and after that Greta had to get out sticky buns and hot chocolate for everybody, since nobody was tired enough to go to bed again.

And so it was a very sleepy group of riders that went out to the stable the next morning to prepare their horses for the final jumping competition.

CHAPTER 14

People already were gathered at the riding ring, and Mia could feel butterflies in her stomach when she looked out through the stable door. Her parents hadn't arrived yet, but Kate's mom and dad, her twin brothers Oscar and Jonathan, and her big sister Theresa, were standing by Prince's stall. Prince seemed very happy with everybody patting him and with all the treats the twins kept feeding him.

Mia had never seen him with his ears forward that long, she thought, stroking Burly's mustard yellow coat. She had given him a bath and a shampoo and cut his close-cropped mane with sharp scissors that she'd borrowed from Emma. For once, she had managed to cut it nice and even, and the black eel-stripe in the middle was very visible.

"Get ready to enter the ring," Greta called into the stable and Mia swallowed.

Her mouth felt dry from nervousness and she needed to go to the bathroom again, although she'd been at least three times in the last half hour.

"Hey, honey."

Mia turned her head and saw her mom and dad.

"I have to go into the ring now," she said, hugging them. "I'm really in a hurry. We can talk later."

"We have a present for you," Mia's dad said with a big smile. "Do you want it now or later?"

"Later," Mia said, running after the others who were already on their way to the ring.

Mia caught up with Linda and Kate, who had started walking around among the obstacles. The obstacles were as tall as houses, she thought, but instead of the old familiar fear she felt a kind of eager anticipation instead. Oh, how she looked forward to flying around this ring on Burly, showing Mom and Dad everything she'd learned in the last five days!

At first the riders walked the course together, and then each by himself or herself, everybody concentrating on the ride a few minutes later. Mia carefully measured the distance between the two final obstacles and quickly realized that this would be a problem for Burly. Would she let him take five or six strides between them? The first obstacle was an oxer and the second an upright post and rail with five white poles.

Mia thought carefully. If he took six short strides instead of five long he would be more collected. That would give him a greater chance of clearing the upright obstacle without knocking down poles, even supposing he came a little close.

Still in her own thoughts, she went back to the stable, saddled and bridled Burly. Her parents were walking around in the big trotting stable with all the other visitors and Mia was glad they weren't disturbing her. This was a big moment for her and Burly, and she felt that she needed to be alone and concentrate.

In the warm-up ring, the starting list was posted. There would be only four riders and horses: Ivy on Samson, Emma on Jolly, Kate with Prince and Mia on Burly. Graygirl and Linda were to jump a lower and easier course and Mistral wouldn't jump at all. He was tender and stiff all over, and when Ricky had walked him a little in the morning, he'd staggered around like an old man.

Mia looked at the starting list again. She hadn't missed anything, she really was starting first, and she realized that she'd better warm up. She concentrated totally on Burly and everything worked out fine. He answered her aids immediately and easily flew over the warm-up obstacles.

Mia slowed and patted his neck. Then she looked over at Greta.

"Are you ready?" Greta called, and Mia answered by nodding. She was more ready than she had ever been, she thought, and rode onto the big jumping course.

The audience was standing by the fence and Mia knew that her parents were somewhere in the group, but she didn't even turn her head when she rode by. She tried to memorize the course instead.

"Okay, you can go," Nick called, and Ricky raised the starting flag. Nick was the judge and timekeeper today.

Mia asked for a gallop, passed the starting line and rode toward the first obstacle, a red and white oxer. It was one of the easiest obstacles on the course and maybe this was why Mia suddenly realized that she and Burly were coming in totally wrong. Instead of letting Burly correct the distance by himself, Mia tried to use the reins to control his stride. Burly jumped way too early and with a big thump the top pole fell to the ground.

Mia felt herself go ice cold inside. She had knocked down the first obstacle! What a catastrophe! Now she wouldn't be able to get to the jump off and show everybody what a great horse Burly was.

With a lump in her throat and tears burning in her eyes she jumped the rest of the course, with no mistakes but with no joy at all. She didn't even notice how Burly did his best and went high above all the other obstacles, and when she reached the finish line, she didn't hear the applause. Instead she just trotted out, patting Burly's neck and trying to keep a smile on her face.

She took the riding jacket off and gave it to Ivy before she let Burly walk up to the stable on long reins.

Inside the stable everything was silent and quiet. Mistral neighed from his stall and Burly answered with a short snort. He looked satisfied when Mia led him into his stall and took his saddle and bridle off. The she slid down into the sawdust, leaned against the wall and let the tears come.

What a failure. And she had been so well prepared, having decided to show everybody that a Fjord horse can certainly jump as well as any other pony. And she had wanted to show her parents what this camp had given her: knowledge, friends and a new assurance that she'd never felt before.

And then there was the rosette. She would get one anyway. Everybody got one, she knew that, but she had wanted to get one by winning. She had imagined it so many times, coming home with a blue rosette, hanging it outside Burly's stall, and…

The tears kept coming and Burly kindly nudged her with his muzzle. "Why are you sitting there feeling sad? Get some hay for me instead!" he seemed to be saying.

Mia drew a shaky breath and stroked his muzzle.

"I know you did your best," she sniffled. "It was my fault that you knocked the obstacle down. I'm sorry!"

At that moment, the door crashed open and Mia heard Kate calling, "Mia! Where are you? You need to jump off."

"What?"

Mia stood up. In the passageway outside the stall were Kate and Prince.

"Yes, everybody's wondering what happened to you. Have you been sitting in here crying? What for? Get your horse out there and warm him up. Greta's rebuilding the course right now, and making all the obstacles higher."

Kate led Prince into his stall and loosened his girth. Mia stared at her, mouth gaping. Then she dried a tear from the corner of her eye and took a deep breath.

"Why are you sad?" Kate asked, looking at her. "Did anything happen?"

"I knocked down the first obstacle! How can we be in the jump off?"

"Jolly refused, Prince and I knocked down three obstacles, and Ivy and Samson missed the last one – so it's you and Ivy in the jump off. You're not going to let her win, are you?"

Mia half ran to the tack room to get her saddle and bridle, and then Kate helped her get Burly ready at top speed. Mia brushed off her riding pants, which were full of sawdust, and Kate doffed her own riding jacket and gave it to her.

"You can use this. The sleeves might be a little short, but who cares. Good luck. I'll keep my fingers crossed for you, until they're all blue!"

"But aren't you disappointed that Prince tore down three poles?" Mia asked when they led Burly out of the stable.

"Oh, who cares," Kate smiled, shrugging her shoulders. "Next time he'll be perfect again. You never know with him. He's a moody horse, and when he doesn't feel like it, it's useless fussing with him."

"Hi! Are you ready?" Greta said when Mia came up to her.

"I just have to warm up a little," Mia breathed, shortening her reins. "Is Ivy ready?"

"Yes, so she gets to start," Nick said. He was standing next to Greta.

"That's not fair," Ivy snorted. "I started last, so I should jump off last, too."

"That's right," Emma chimed in.

She was standing next to Jolly, who was half asleep, with his ears straight out and resting one hind leg.

"If it's going to be like a real competition, let's make it like a real competition," she went on, tossing her head.

Mia thought that Emma seemed to have recovered quickly from her boy troubles yesterday. Greta looked at Mia, who took a deep breath.

"Okay, I can start first, but I have to warm Burly up first," she said. "It would be unfair if I didn't."

"So why did you untack, stupid?" Emma said. "Why didn't you wait until everybody had jumped?"

"Get going then, instead of standing here jabbering," Ivy said, and Mia felt herself getting angry, as usual. She was going to show those two bigheads. She was sure that they'd thought that one of them was going to win when Burly knocked down the first obstacle, but she was going to show them it wasn't that easy.

Mia rode for a while, calm and concentrated. She tried not to hurry too much, although Emma and Ivy were standing at the warm-up ring and several times Emma said loudly that this would have to be enough. Mia took Burly over one of the warm-up obstacles one more time before she nodded to Greta.

"We're ready."

Greta smiled and opened the gate to the ring. Ricky took his place at the starting line and Nick gave the signal.

Now the course was shorter and the obstacles were higher, but Mia could feel joy bubbling up inside her. She had gotten a second chance, and she was going to use it. She asked Burly to gallop and rode toward the red and white oxer again. This time Burly flew over it in a high and beautiful jump, and Mia felt herself going dizzy with happiness.

The rest of the course went equally well. Once again, she had the feeling of riding in a dream, and Burly cleared obstacle after obstacle without even touching them.

The two last obstacles were placed in a tricky way. There was a tight turn before the first one, and then there was the post and rail she had worried so much about before. Mia wasn't really sure if she should choose a shorter path and take the risk of knocking down the obstacle or if she should let Burly run the curve wide and come in right for both obstacles.

For a fraction of a second she was close to riding the fastest path, but then she ran the curve a little wider and came in exactly right for the blue and yellow oxer. Then she collected Burly, making him as short as she could, and he took exactly six strides before soaring above the post and rail. After the obstacle, he quickly galloped to the finish line, and Mia patted his neck, bursting with joy. He had made a clear round!

They walked out from the ring, and at the gate they met Ivy. Ivy looked determined and rode Samson with short reins. He eagerly jig-jogged and tossed his head to get longer reins. Ivy snorted something at him and then rode onto the course in a slow, bouncy canter.

She got her starting signal almost at once and as soon as Ricky raised the flag Ivy let Samson go for the first obstacle. Samson flew high above it and turned for the next one while he was still in the air.

Ivy was perfectly balanced with her pony and Samson was experienced enough to be able to jump in any situation. He cleared obstacle after obstacle without hesitating for a second, and although he was already running fast he seemed to want to move even faster. He threw himself at several of the obstacles while Ivy did all she could to keep him calm.

When the two last obstacles came up, Ivy did exactly the kind of tight and cool turn that Mia herself had wanted to do, and Mia took a breath. Ivy earned a lot of time and Mia realized that she had met her match. But it didn't matter that much anymore. She had gotten her chance to show what they could do, and she felt satisfied when she patted Burly's neck.

"Here's today's winner," Nick said when Ivy and Samson had crossed the finish line, and Mia knew that they had made a much better time than she.

"Way to go!" Ricky called to Ivy when she and Samson trotted for the exit, and Ivy smiled back, happy with her round.

"Fast but not very elegant," Kate mumbled, winking encouragingly at Mia before she disappeared to rebuild the course for Linda and Graygirl.

"You're the best horse in the world," Mia smiled, hugging Burly. "We've never jumped this high before."

"Yes, it's not bad to come in second in this group," Greta said, suddenly standing next to Mia.

"Not at all," Mia said, smiling. "I'm very happy."

"Where did you go after the first round?" Greta said. "Did you put him in the stable?"

Mia nodded.

"Yes, I thought we were done, so I felt I might as well do that."

Greta smiled at her, and suddenly Mia realized that she knew exactly how it felt, and how disappointed Mia had been after knocking down that first obstacle.

"Never give up until the last rider is done," she said, winking as if she and Mia shared a secret before she went to help Nick rebuild the course for Linda and Graygirl.

A little later, it was their turn, and Graygirl went

around the course with ease. Linda rode her calmly, and when they came to the finish line she got the longest round of applause for the day from a little bow-legged man in his sixties, dressed in worn jeans, a shirt with short sleeves and a cap with the logo of one of the big trotting tracks.

"Grandpa," Linda called, sliding down from Graygirl and hugging the man, who was standing with a woman that Mia could tell was Linda's mom. "You came!"

"Well, I had to see what you're doing with the poor horse," Linda's grandpa muttered, a little embarrassed, and Mia could hear in his voice how happy he was.

"Time to give out the prizes!" Nick called and everybody got ready. Marching music came from the speakers while they rode onto the course: Ivy and Samson, Mia and Burly, Kate (who was walking, since Prince was in his stall in the stable), Emma and Jolly and finally Linda and Graygirl.

Everybody got a rosette and Mia thought that the red one that Nick attached to Burly's bridle was the most beautiful one she'd ever seen. The fact that she got to ride her lap of honor as second, after Ivy and Samson, didn't matter in the least. She was so happy she could have run the lap of honor herself. Over and over again, she patted Burly's neck and praised him.

Burly turned an ear back to listen to her, and Mia was sure he understood how happy and satisfied she was with him.

CHAPTER 15

About an hour later, it was time to go home. Mia had put the trailer guards on Burly, but no blanket. It was much too hot for that today.

"Where's the car?" Mia asked her dad, and he pointed to the parking area.

"Over there," he said. "Come on!"

"What if he doesn't want to go in?" Mom said in a nervous voice. "He was good when we were coming here, but you never know, now that we're going home."

"Mom," Mia said in a commanding voice, "go to the tack room and grab our saddle. And don't come out until Burly is in the trailer."

Her mom gave her a surprised look. Then she smiled and walked toward the stable.

"Not bad for our little girl," Mia's dad said, patting her shoulder. "I think you've learned to stand up for yourself."

"Oh," Mia smiled, "we all know Burly will walk right in. She just worries him. Come on. Where's this trailer you rented?"

"It's ours!" Dad said proudly, and Mia stared at him.

"You bought a trailer?" she exclaimed. "Are you out of your mind? They're so expensive!"

"I got this one cheap from the Nilssons in town. Both his kids quit riding and they sold their horses. I simply swapped this trailer for hay for his calves. I've already gotten almost all our hay in, and it's all looking great."

"That's good," Mia laughed.

"Yes, and a friend of mine said that they have jumping classes at the riding school in town every Saturday. Now we can go there with Burly," Mom said, coming out with Burly's saddle and bucket.

Mia stared at them with eyes as big as saucers.

"I don't get it," she muttered suspiciously. "You never wanted to do that kind of stuff before. Does this have something to do with school?"

"Well, of course we've wanted you to practice. You're

the one who's always been unsure," Dad said, putting his hand on Mia's shoulder.

"No way!" Mia exclaimed. "Not with the way I've been begging to go to a riding school."

Mom put the saddle in the car and came back to them.

"Do you remember last fall when you rode at the school with Burly? You went there once but never again."

Mia blushed and looked down. She remembered how terrible it had felt that only time she'd ridden in the indoor riding ring in town. She had thought that everybody was staring at her, that she was the worst rider, and…

Suddenly she realized that in a way, her parents were right. It was true that she'd dreamed about training, but she'd never really dared to take the chance. And she'd probably never have been in a competition if Tessa hadn't nagged her into it.

Now she realized that it was her own shyness and fear of making a fool of herself that had stopped her from trying. Now that obstacle was gone. These five days had taught her that she could trust herself and her own ability to get through things. And in that moment, it was as if a heavy burden were lifted from her shoulders and had just disappeared into thin air.

"Thanks a lot. You're the best," Mia said, hugging her mom and then her dad. "Now let's get Burly in!"

At that moment, Kate came running over. She threw hers arms around Mia's neck and hugged her tightly.

"Bye. Promise you'll write! I'll come to see you later this summer."

Kate's mom was coming closer, driving the car with a trailer attached. Everyone standing there could hear the kicks and thuds from within, and Kate let go of Mia and ran over to the car.

"Have to leave now before Prince kicks the trailer to pieces! Bye for now," she yelled, jumping into the car, which immediately rolled out of the yard.

Mia looked after it and smiled. Prince's hind hooves were kicking at the wall, and she realized that Prince Sourpuss was in a very bad mood.

Mia held Burly while Dad lowered the ramp of the trailer. Then Burly walked in, without the slightest fuss, and began eating the hay inside. Mia tied him up and jumped out through the front door. She still couldn't fathom that this was hers, and that this was the present Dad had been talking about. It was too good to be true!

A honking car horn woke her from her reveries and Linda's grandpa stopped his car right next to her. Linda rolled her window down.

"Did I give you my address?"

"Yes, you certainly did," Mia said, laughing. "I have it written down in at least three places!"

"Good," Linda said merrily. "See you later in the summer, then. Now I'm going home to practice, so we can be in competitions this fall."

"You do that," Mia said. "See you!"

Linda waved as her grandpa started the car again, and soon they too were gone.

"It seems you've made lots of new friends this week," Mia's mom said, putting her arm around Mia's shoulders for a little hug.

"Yes," Mia said, a little embarrassed. "Linda and Kate are my best friends, and I've gotten to know a girl named Angelica, too. She bought Mistral – he used to belong to Ricky, but Ricky wants a bigger horse now. And Mistral got stuck in a marsh, and then –"

"Let's go home already!" Dad said, laughing. "You can tell us on the way."

All three got in the car and soon they were driving homeward. Mia looked at the well-tended fences and the slender brown horses that were grazing at the side of the drive, but when the car turned onto the highway she leaned back and closed her eyes.

She hardly knew where to begin, telling her parents everything. Such incredible things had happened, and the memories flew by inside her. The practice sessions, the long trail ride, Mistral's running off which ended in the marsh, the boy-girl melodrama, and then of course that little matter about the fire alarm.

Mia yawned and stretched. Now, finally, she felt how tired she was after five days of excitement. Before she knew it, she was fast asleep with the red rosette in her hand.